NOBODY'S CHILD

SARAH'S STORY

K. Moody Hoskins

ISBN 978-1-0980-9345-7 (paperback)
ISBN 978-1-0980-9346-4 (digital)

Christian Faith Publishing, Inc.
832 Park Avenue
Meadville, PA 16335
www.christianfaithpublishing.com

Printed in the United States of America

Inspired by a True Story

"Sometimes young folks chase dreams that
are not what the good Lord intended."
                                            —Doc Southall

Acknowledgments

This book is dedicated to the memory of Patty Jean Parker—a woman of God, a mother, a grandmother, a sister, an auntie, a cousin, a friend, a quintessential Black Queen.

Aunt Jean,

You didn't know it, but you were the female idol of my childhood. You were the vivacious, spirited icon of flavor whose magnetic energy became indelibly imprinted on my young impressionable heart. Growing up, you were the one whose magic I was fascinated by and reveled in whenever you were around. It was you I wanted to model as I grew into an adult. I realize now, that in many ways, I'm a product of that influence. It's helped me keep an open mind—to not be afraid of trying new things, to be adventurous and daring. By your example, I learned, no matter your age, everything is made easier when you're having fun!

Sadly, those defining days in my youth, when you were so much a part of our lives, were cut short. Decades would pass with no mention, no word, and without us knowing why. Then one day, out of nowhere, there was a phone call. I will always be thankful for the opportunity we were given to say a last goodbye. The memory of the day Joan and I visited will stay with me forever.

That was the day you shared your story and provided answers to so much. All our lives, we had known you as an aunt when, really, you were our cousin. Finally, it all made sense. I understand why the book you imagined based on your life you titled *Nobody's Child*.

Families are often complicated, and what may not be obvious to young children can be a compilation of years of adult history riddled with misunderstandings. Nevertheless, I wish we could have had more time. The conversations we could have had. The questions I would have asked. The good times and laughter there would have been.

This is probably not the story you imagined, but it's the one I was led to write. This book is a work of fiction fueled by a broad understanding of the circumstances that surrounded your birth. Armed with that framework, this writer's imagination took over and ultimately directed what got on the page. Only you could have told the accurate story of a life that was so complex, repudiated, and troubled.

In the same way, all things work together for a purpose. I believe hearing your story that day was connected with mine and was a parting gift from you to me. For that, I will be forever grateful. Writing this book has been a labor of love, and I hope it makes you proud.

Love,
Karen

Patty Jean Parker
April 28, 1931–December 16, 2012

Chapter 1

June 1943

"No, wait! Don't do it!" Rita screamed, but thirteen-year-old Sarah ignored the warning and focused her eyes keenly on the rope ahead and prepared to sprint toward it. Five boys and two other girls from school stood watching in the hot sun on the riverbank, waiting to see what she would do next. Loudmouthed Roger made the dare, saying girls were weak and not strong enough to handle the Mahoning Crusher.

The Crusher, a well-known locally manufactured thrill ride, involved a running start to then jump six feet from the bank in order to catch a twisted rope that hung from the extended branch of a big oak tree. The trick, though, was to hold on tight, swing out wide over the flowing water twenty feet below, and swing back. Before that day, no girl had ever attempted the feat. It was just one of those things immature young boys did to entertain themselves on warm summer afternoons in the small Midwestern town of Warren, Ohio.

They took turns at the rope, bragging to each other and trying to impress the three girls who came to watch. The ones who successfully made the dangerous journey over the river and back were celebrated like heroes. But others who slipped and fell into the rushing Mahoning River below became the target of jokes; when soaked, they climbed back up the rocky cliff to the top of the bank. But on the return, some would land short of the bank and slam hard against the rocky side. Since last summer, two boys ended up with broken arms, and another fractured his collarbone.

"The Crusher is for *men!*" Roger yelled when he once again landed both feet steady on the ground on his return swing. Letting go of the rope, he pounded his chest with pride, like he was Tarzan.

As if you were a man, Sarah thought to herself, rolling her eyes.

"Girls are too weak to handle the Crusher!" he said overly expressive, accusingly pointing his index finger at the female classmates watching him.

"Shut up, Roger! You don't know what you're talking about!" Sarah shouted back.

"I bet I can do it. Girls are just as strong as you stupid boys!" She was infuriated by his comment and ignited by the idea of a challenge to prove he was wrong.

"Let me at that rope!"

Rita repeatedly pleaded for her not to do it. But just like always, she didn't listen—she never did.

Fortunately, Sarah didn't break an arm or her collarbone that day. But on the return swing back to the bank, her grip on the rope slipped, causing her to crash against the side. A jagged rock that was sticking out caught the top of her right thigh and scraped it badly. She winced with pain when it happened. Blood appeared quickly. It stained her white Bermuda shorts and ran down her leg. Clawing and struggling at the rope, miraculously, she found the strength to pull herself back up on the cliff. Once safe on solid ground, she grabbed at her leg, clutching it in pain. She had the scare of her life! But despite being bloody and hurting, she managed a smile, pleased with knowing she had made her point.

⌘

Children in Warren attended Saint Bernadette's Covenant School on the edge of town. It was the only school in the county between there and West Farmington. If local children got an education, that's where they went, whether their families were practicing Catholics or not—except, of course, for the colored children.

It was a strict curriculum based on scriptural principles and no-nonsense—which coincidentally also included reading, writing, and arithmetic. Teen girls wore polyester pleated, plaid skirts, a simple cardigan sweater over a Peter Pan—collared blouse, topped off by white bobby socks and Mary Jane shoes. The boys dressed in dark high-waisted cotton-blend pants with white collared shirts and penny loafers.

There were separate classrooms for girls and boys, and the two were separated in between by a darkened narrow hallway. Sister Anne was the girls' teacher, and Sister Martha taught the boys. In her austere voice, Head Mother repeated the same mantra to the girls on the first day of school every year: "Sister Bernadette young ladies will not be the objects of the mischievous *tinkerings* of immature adolescent boys."

The girls didn't understand what *tinkerings* meant, but no one ever got up the nerve to ask her. They were also curious about what she told the boys when later she delivered a similar opening day lecture in their classroom down the hall. Head Mother's face was pale and stony and framed tightly by the coif that wrapped and covered her head. During morning Bible study, scripture recitation, and prayer, she walked back and forth between the two classrooms, peeking in through the square window in the door, observing if students were paying attention. If she saw any of them staring off into space, the way young people do, she would interrupt the class and direct the nun to assign extra verses for that student to memorize for the next day. Her long black habit flowed wide as she patrolled the hallway between the classrooms like a sentry guard. She was determined to make sure "the little devils," as she called them, minded their "Ps and Qs" while under her watch.

By age fifteen, Sarah was becoming more mature and putting aside her earlier tomboy ways. The inherent beauty passed on from Lucy, her mother, was taking root and evolving into a maturity that brought with it a subtle yet distinct allure that had begun to attract the attention of males. Her no-fear attitude from early adolescence was emerging as an inward strength, a budding confidence. She could hold her own in conversations with adults and be assertive in giving her opinion, whether it was solicited or not. More than once, she was sent to Head Mother's office after Sister ordered her to leave the classroom for "speaking out of turn." Often it was because she complained out loud about the homework they had to do.

"Sister, how are we supposed to get all this done in one evening! We've got chores to do when we get home." Routinely, she was the advocate for the rest of the class. But her sassiness only got her into trouble. Adults found it peculiarly annoying for a young girl to be so plainspoken. Teenagers were only to be seen and certainly not heard, which was just one of the many traditional values that defined small-town life in Warren and everywhere else in Ohio, for that matter. The older she got, traditionalism became a major source of her adolescent frustration. It fueled her desire to escape to someplace less limiting and where people were open to new ideas.

Sister Anne took an interest in Sarah after Lucy's death. Watching her mother sick for months, and then die from cancer, sent Sarah into an emotional spiral. The already confident young girl became defiant and angry and even quicker-tongued and sassy. Sister Anne, a fortysomething-aged nun, was empathetic to her pain and tried to be supportive of the quick-spoken, flighty girl, who had no mother to guide her on the path to becoming a woman. The two first bonded one day after school when quiet, rosy-cheeked Sister Anne stayed late to help Sarah with her report on Mary Magdalene.

All the other students had gone for the day, so Sister Anne sat next to Sarah in one of the student desks. Covered from head to toe in white robing, she cramped herself oddly into the small wooden seat.

"You're a smart young lady. It's nice to see that in a girl your age," said Sister. She reached over and grabbed Sarah's hand to stop her pencil from writing. Sarah was startled by the gesture and turned and looked up at her.

"No man wants a wife who doesn't have a good head on her." Sister tightened the grasp on Sarah's hand to emphasize her point.

Sarah's stomach knotted inside. She looked away and back down at her paper. She hated when older women lectured her that way. As if wife and mother were the only dreams she was allowed to have. It was all she could do to contain her feelings and not lash out.

"Sarah Ruford, you must keep your head on your shoulders and out of the clouds. Both your feet must be firmly planted on the ground, young lady!" Sister tapped sharply on the desk with her index finger.

"That is, of course, if you want to find a good man and raise a family. And every young girl wants to have that, right?"

The nun leaned in toward her and waited for a response to confirm that they were in agreement. But the typically opinionated Sarah kept her head down and simmered in the dislike of what Sister had said. Sister Anne was trying to be of support, but Sarah couldn't help but resent the mediocre existence she had just described as being her dream life. Though she said nothing, she dreamed of the day when she would be able to show her she had done much more with her life than just becoming someone's wife and tending to home and family.

Slender and taller than most boys her age, Sarah's long legs arrived at their destination before the rest of her. She had eyes of the Bette Davis variety that were like deep ponds of blue. They were eyes rich with curiosity and the effervescence of youth.

Although still a teen, when she entered a room, something uncanny that was intangible but distinct caught your attention. A bold innocence that was beyond description. Perhaps it was her youthful sureness or the contagious energy she seemed to radiate or the coy, naive schoolgirl giggle she let go whenever something was funny—and which helped remind adults that she was still just a child. It could also have been the way her ponytail swung playfully side to side when she walked or even how natural strands of golden in her sandy hair complemented so nicely the pink tones of her cheeks. Maybe it was how her eyes sometimes flickered green or the way the dimple in her left cheek made everything seem brighter when she smiled. Whatever it was, Sarah was singular in design, charmingly odd, a rare find, and a true beauty in a natural, earthy sort of way. A young jewel, living in a rural, placid town, with a budding potential to shine.

Chapter 2

Sarah's time and attention growingly became obsessed with fashion magazines and the models featured in them. She was consumed with fantasies about the exciting lives they must live. Elizabeth Gibbons and Dana Jenney were among her idols, and she loved the straighter-fitted styles they were wearing. Every third Thursday, the monthly magazines were dropped at Fisher's Pharmacy, where she worked after school and during the summer. During her break, she sat at the Formica lunch counter, devouring the pages of *Vogue* magazine and imagining herself, like the models, posing for photographs and looking glamourous. She sat there engrossed, twirling thick strands of her ponytail around two fingers—oblivious to anyone and anything, except what was on the page. She envied the young women in their makeup and designer clothes, posing on the streets of Manhattan. In her daydreams, they had lots of money and lived in luxurious Park Avenue apartments. They went to fancy parties and surrounded themselves with wealthy businessmen and artsy types. She imagined that life and not the limited one she had living in a dopey town in Ohio with its two churches (Catholic and Methodist) and a sawmill. In New York, she would enjoy the social life of a model, meet and one day marry a millionaire, and they would live in a big flat on the Upper East Side. Eventually, two beautiful, perfect children would arrive: a boy and a girl. Of course, there would be a maid and a nanny to take care of them so that she could make daily appointments for photo work and runway jobs. She was bursting with ambition and delusional about a life she could only imagine but was desperate to discover. If she was ever to have the life she wanted, she knew it meant finding a way to get far away from Warren.

Truth was, people didn't typically leave Warren. Her mother, like some others, had tried but failed and eventually gave up and just resigned themselves as satisfied with life in a small town. Even most of the young men in town who left to fight in the war came back home after their tours were done. They settled down and raised a family like you were supposed to do. Sarah's restlessness and persistent conversation about getting as far away from Warren as she could became a nuisance to many of the locals. When helping customers check out and pay for their items at the pharmacy cash register, she ranted on and on, to anyone who would listen, about her big-city dreams and how she was going to be famous someday.

"You'll see, Mr. Ragland, one day, I'll be famous and make everybody in this town proud of my success!" she told the owner of the feed store one day.

Around town, she became known as the brash schoolgirl with the ridiculous notion of moving to the city. Eager and ready for change, she vowed to do whatever it took to see what else there was beyond Warren. To do that, she would need money and a plan.

It was May 1948, and a ninth-grade education was more than enough for any able-bodied American to get a job. Having just turned seventeen in April, and with the school year ending, Sarah made up in her mind she had gotten all the education she needed and that it was time to get on with her life. She was an average student, but arithmetic and reading were her best subjects. Packard Electric was expanding and building a new plant just five miles outside town. They were hiring, and with her knack for numbers, she would have no problem getting a job as a clerk in the office. Warren was buzzing with talk about the good-paying jobs that were coming. But the thought of a routine job in an office offered her no motivation. Even the mention of the word "clerk" rebuffed at her insides.

❧

After her mother died, Sarah was basically left to raise herself in the same small house where they lived with Lucy's younger brother, Brady. They were poor and struggled to pay their bills. Brady had his own issues, not the least of which were women and liquor. He had never married or, for that matter, kept a girlfriend for very long. He told Lucy once, "There's just too many pretty girls on planet Earth for me to pick just one."

Approaching fifty, Brady Ruford was strong, rugged, and earthy. He was a chiseled, country, six feet two, with wild curly blond hair that always tended to be out of control and in need of a cut. He was handsome and had the family's crystal-blue eyes. But his sight was bad. So bad, in fact, that he was classified IV-F by the military, which made him ineligible for the draft. Without his wire-rim glasses, he could see very little. His wit was sharp, which made him easy to like. Town folks knew if you ran into Brady, there was the guarantee of a joke and probably the faint smell of whiskey on his breath. His temper was fast, and if pushed too far, he didn't run from a fight. He was reactive in defending his white liberal ideas, which didn't always fit with Midwestern values and certainly not in a town where there were known to be Klannish people and bigoted conversations. More than once, Sheriff Pike had driven him home in the squad car, drunk and beaten up from a fight he most likely started.

"When your uncle sobers up, tell him next time he'll be keeping company overnight with me in the jailhouse," the sheriff said gruffly, one Friday night after Sarah opened the door. The sheriff wore a frown and looked angry as he stood there in his gray uniform, holding drunk, black-eyed, and bruised Brady up by one arm.

"Yes, sir, I'll tell him."

Sarah put her shoulder up under her uncle's arm and helped him stumble into the house.

⁂

"As long as you find a job, it's fine by me," Brady said the evening she told him she didn't want to go back to school. She was sprinkling Morton's Salt in the chicken stew she was making for their dinner when he came through the kitchen door. He was a carpenter, and his clothes were dirty and covered in sawdust, his face tired and drawn from working all day. She knew he would be dog tired but couldn't wait to tell him.

"You've already been farther in school than me or your mama. Jobs at Packard should be opening up soon. Maybe you can get hired on there?" His voice dragged with exhaustion. He took a seat at the table, leaned down, and began loosing the laces of his left boot.

The two of them had a relationship that was deeply grounded in family, but they lived together more like roommates, each separately going about their daily routines. Yet Sarah knew her uncle's love for her was fierce and that she could count on him if ever she needed him.

"No, I don't want to work at the plant, Uncle Brady!" she said, candid. She could feel herself standing up for herself like an adult and not a kid anymore. And it felt good.

"Why not? They'll be paying good money." He pulled the boot off his foot and started loosening the laces of the other one.

"Working there is not how I want to spend the rest of my life, Uncle Brady! I can't sit at a desk all day!" She shrugged and showed her frustration, still stirring at the pot of stew.

"This isn't about you wanting to be some kinda fashion model, is it?" he asked, joking but curious. "Is your head still full of that nonsense?"

Sarah waited a few seconds to respond, knowing he would never be able to understand.

"Yeah, it's my dream!" she blurted, as though needing to defend the idea. "I'm going to be in magazines, and people all over the world are going to recognize my face." She continued to stir the stew but pulled her shoulders back, pushed out her chest and tilted her chin sharply up, in a pose that mimicked the sophisticated glamour of the person she someday hoped to be.

"You want to do what!" Laughing, Brady removed his dusty red baseball cap and ran his hand front to back through his wild hair.

"The job and the life I want can't happen as long as I stay trapped here in Warren. I have to get out of here, Uncle Brady!"

Brady slapped his cap back on and chuckled under his breath.

"All right, Lucy Girl. I can't wait to see how this plan of yours turns out."

Lucy Girl was the nickname he began calling her after his sister died. She and Brady were born Irish twins and couldn't have been closer. He missed her. Sarah reminded him of her in every way. Both were headstrong and tough, and once they got an idea stuck in their heads, there was little point in arguing to change their minds.

The Ruford house was a local hangout. All sorts of random townspeople showed up on the front porch, looking to have a drink and a good laugh with Brady. Their house became so popular that on Saturday nights, Brady started collecting fifty cents at the door. It wasn't much, but the extra money helped buy food and oil for the tank, which was a must for the winter cold. By 10:00 p.m., it wasn't uncommon for thirty people to be jammed downstairs between the front room and hallway of their aging two-bedroom clapboard house listening and dancing to music or playing cards at the table in their cramped kitchen, the gang of them drinking, smoking, and having a good time. Brady moved the couch and end tables against the wall next to his grandmother's piano. When he put "The Duke" on the Victrola, the hardwood floors scuffled with the sound of couples dancing to the rhythm of swing, colored and whites alike, all dancing together and loving the music. But that was the Ruford house—a place where all were welcome and no one was judged.

A well-known local musician, Brady could sit down at the piano and navigate his way through almost any song. Music was one of the main reasons he had so many Negro friends. He liked the same jazz and blues they did. Charlie Parker, Dizzy Gillespie, and Billie Holiday topped his list of favorites. Some weekends, instead of pay-to-enter Saturday-night parties at the house, he played piano for tips with some of the colored musicians at the Negro bar about three miles from town. They were always glad to see Brady whenever he showed up. The crowd was awed and amazed to watch a white man play with so much soul.

One humid Saturday night in late June, Sarah was at the house in her usual spot—sitting in one of the kitchen chairs, next to the open, screened front door. It was her job to collect the house fee whenever one of the locals showed up, an empty Maxwell House coffee can in her lap to collect the fifty cents admission—and it was clanking with change. While she waited, she flipped through an old copy of *Vogue* and waited to see who else might appear on their weathered old porch. Overtime, she had acquired a huge collection of the magazine, and she never tired of getting lost in even the old copies.

"Evening, Miss Sarah."

It was Charles, the colored trumpet player from the bar. He emerged out of the night and onto the porch suddenly. The light coming from a single bulb over the door was bright and shining down on his gray fedora hat. Insects attracted by the light swarmed around his head.

"Hi, Charles!" She sounded young, bubbly, and happy to see him. "How's Odessa?" she asked excitedly.

Charles's daughter, Odessa, was a year younger than Sarah. When they were little, Odessa would sometimes come to the house with Charles, and he and Brady would practice music together. She was a precocious little girl with intense brown eyes and ebony black skin. The two of them played and had fun up in Sarah's room, and while Lucy was at work, they tried on her makeup and hats. Downstairs, her poppa and Brady created soulful bluesy sounds that filled the house.

"She's fine, Miss Sarah."

Charles peered his neck past her and through the screen, trying to see who else was inside.

"I'm sorry, Charles. It's fifty cents to come inside, and that goes for everybody."

"No problem, Miss Sarah. I got your money right here."

He dug in his pocket, pulled out two coins, and dropped them in the can.

"All right, well, come on in." She smiled and giggled when she held the door open, and he walked past her.

By midnight, no one had shown up on the porch for nearly an hour. She hadn't counted the money yet, but by looking at the coins in the bottom of the can, her guess was there was about eight dollars. She looked past the people scattered around the front room and back into the kitchen, where Brady sat at the head of the table, playing poker with three of his friends. He must have just said something funny because his friends were pointing at him and laughing. Smoke from their cigarettes had collected around the long fluorescent light that hung over the table, and it cast a haze around the room. The game was obviously exciting because a few others were standing around the table, drinks in hand, watching. Sarah raised a hand high in the air and waved it back and forth with the intention for Brady to see. He immediately noticed and responded with a few affirming nods of his head in her direction. It was their sign that she was closing the door, taking the coffee can up to her room and going to bed.

That night, Vernon Schiffle had finished off one too many Budweisers. He was making a nuisance of himself, stumbling around and bumping into people. Eventually, he made his way over to the banister and was standing there, wobbly, holding onto the wooden rail, when Sarah passed him on her way up the steps. She caught his attention, and he began following her every movement, step by step, staring at her as though in a trance. Without notice, Vernon's inhibitions took leave of him and cagey, he followed up the steps behind her. Just as Sarah was turning the knob to open her bedroom door, he grabbed her around the waist from behind. She reacted, startled, but before she could scream, he put his smelly hand over her mouth and wrestled her through the open door and onto the bed. Cab Calloway's "Conga" was blaring from the turntable. No one heard or had a clue what was happening upstairs.

Sarah kicked and fought, trying to scream, but Vernon clamped his hand over her mouth even tighter. They struggled, but he managed to slip his other hand inside the top of her pants. He yanked at her body until he got them down and over her feet. She battled hard and furious like a cat, scratching and pulling at him. She was more angry than scared.

Calling on all her strength, she took her right hand and dug the nails of her fingers into the skin of his cheek, until it drew blood. He pulled back in pain but kept one hand over her mouth and grabbed at the wound on his flushed red face with the other. It didn't much stop him, though, as he fumbled to loosen his belt.

"Don't fight me, you sweet gal," he slurred.

His breath smelled of liquor and Camel cigarettes, and his body was funky like he had worked and sweated all day but hadn't bathed. Sarah's heart raced as she thought of losing her virginity to this man she barely knew and who was old enough to be her father. When the record on the Victrola ended, she bit his hand hard, causing him to release the hold over her mouth. When he let go, she screamed loud and desperate. The people downstairs let out a collective gasp when they heard it.

Brady heard the scream and jerked in the direction of her room. He flung the cards he was holding in his hand across the table and turned over his chair, frantically rushing to get up. Pushing people out of the way, he ran two, sometimes three, steps at a time, up the stairs. When he got to Sarah's room and saw Vernon forcing himself on her, he lost it.

"You bastard! What the hell are you doing!"

Brady grabbed Vernon by the back of the collar and pulled him off her and onto the floor. He began kicking him with his boots and punching him in the face, out of control. The slapping sound of his fists against Vernon's face was so intense, Sarah thought he was going to kill him. On one of the blows, Brady's glasses flew off his face and onto the floor. She scurried to get them. Quickly, she pulled up her pants, skimmed around the two of them scuffling and ran out of the room.

"Come help, he's killing him!" she yelled down the steps to the crowd below. They were frozen, waiting to know what was going on.

Claude, another one of Brady's friends, and Charles ran up the stairs and into the room and began trying to pull him off Vernon.

"Let me go, I'm going to kill this SOB!"

"Come on, buddy, you don't want to do that," Claude said as he and Charles each grabbed one of Brady's arms, pulling him off Vernon and over to the other side of the room. Brady was strong,

23

and it was all they could do to hold him. When he eventually started calming down, Charles, seeing the beating Brady had given him, let go and went and tried to help Vernon to his feet.

"Get your nigga hands off me," Vernon said, snatching his arm away, his lip busted and a nasty gash bleeding over his left eye.

"I'm trying to save your no-good life. You need to get up out of here before Brady bashes your head in some more," said Charles.

Bloody and moving with pain, Vernon got up, holding his stomach, and staggered slowly out of the room and down the stairs. The Saturday-night crowd kept quiet when they saw him, his face bloody and battered. They moved to get out of his way, and he stumbled out the front door.

"Let me go!" Brady said, angry.

He shook himself from the hold Claude still had on him. Twice he ran his hand front to back through his wiry blond hair to get it out of his face. The punches he delivered on Vernon had been so hard, his right fist was visibly red and beginning to swell. He rubbed at it to soothe the pain. Meanwhile, Sarah, still stunned, sat knees to her chest on the floor just outside the door in the hall. She had listened to the rest of the skirmish but didn't go back inside.

"The party is over! Tell those good-for-nothings downstairs to get the hell out of my house!" yelled Brady.

Claude and Charles gave each other a questioning look and then left the room and went downstairs.

Brady came out to see Sarah sitting on the floor, pressed against the wall. She looked up at him, her eyes wide and staring. "What made him do that, Uncle Brady?" Her voice was blatant with anger and confusion.

Brady didn't answer. He squatted down in front of her, felt around her hand to find his glasses, and put them on. He put his hand to her chin and turned her head from side to side, examining it to see if she had been hurt. When she appeared not to be harmed, he exhaled and sat down on the floor beside her and pulled her head to his chest.

"I'm so sorry, Lucy Girl. It's my fault for letting this happen. I told your mama I would take care of you. But I promise you, I won't let anything like this ever happen to you again! You hear me?" Brady held her tight.

The front door closed with a thump, and the house became quiet. They sat together on the floor with him holding her close several more minutes, neither of them saying a word. But Sarah played the incident over and over in her head…

I almost lost my virginity—and to Vernon!

She was repulsed by what could have been.

"Uncle Brady, you didn't answer me. Why did Vernon go crazy like that?"

"Well, Lucy Girl, you're what some men call a 'looker.'" He took his hand and wiped away the strands of hair that had fallen in her face.

"A pretty girl can sometimes make a man do stupid things, Sarah. Vernon had too many tonight, and his manhood got the best of him."

Sarah still didn't really understand what made him go off like that. But she chose not to ask any more questions. By the age of sixteen, she had kissed two boys. The first time was Hank Carter behind St. Bernadette's after school one day. She had had a crush on him since fifth grade, so in the seventh, when clumsily his lips touched hers, it was a dream come true. The second time was two years later down at the river, under the oak tree, with the gang from school. Three of the boys—Frank, Roger, and Clyde—dared her to hold a kiss with Otis for sixty seconds while they counted it down.

"Fifteen, sixteen, seventeen, eighteen," the boys clamored loud and in unison. Sarah thought the seconds dragged on forever. She didn't care about Otis, but she couldn't turn away from a dare, so she held her lips pressed to his for the whole minute. But Vernon was the first time she had done anything anywhere near close to losing her virginity. She felt oddly changed by what had happened. Like one of those rare moments in youth, when in an instant, the chapter on childhood is closed, and a door opens to what's next—a strange type of growth spurt. It had been the first time a male had touched her in that way. But it wouldn't be the last.

Chapter 3

The following Friday, Sarah eavesdropped from the front room, as she often did, while Brady and three of his buddies drank, smoked cigarettes, and played rummy at the kitchen table. She leaned in close from the hallway door as they went on with boisterous conversation about everything from the draft to whether the Cleveland Indians would make it to the series or not. "There's no stopping that DiMaggio. Those boys are headed for the pennant again this year. You watch what I say!" Ralph was the only Yankees fan in the bunch.

That evening, they were also laughing and talking about a place in Youngstown where they had gone a few weeks before. From what Sarah could hear, she concluded that it was a place where ladies entertained, and men drank and had a good time. She moved her ear closer to the door.

"Man, that girl was so pretty she could have taken all my money, and I would have given it to her too…and with a big-ol' smile!" Brady said, studying his hand. He joked while shaking his head in disbelief. The others looked up over their cards and laughed aloud!

"I need to save my money so I can go back," said Claude. "That colored lady at the desk charged me four dollars!"

That sounds like a place where girls make a lot of money! Sarah got excited just thinking about the possibilities.

"Whites and coloreds having a good time under the same roof, never thought I would see the day." Charles rearranged the cards in his hand.

Maybe they're showgirls, she thought, remembering a picture she once saw in *Vogue*. Ladies were dancing in high heels in a chorus line wearing cute, skimpy costumes.

That wouldn't be so bad and maybe even fun, especially if it paid a lot of money. She squinted and considered the idea.

Besides, I wouldn't do it for long. When I have enough money, I can leave this stupid town.

Sarah fell back gently against the wall to not let on that she was listening. Rolling her eyes up at the ceiling, she wallowed in how badly she wanted to leave Warren. She thought about Lucy and how she never got the life she wanted.

Mama, you'll be able to live your dream through me. I'm getting us both out of here!

She closed her eyes and squeezed them tight, thinking of her mother's pain at knowing she would never see what else there was in the world. Moving back close to the door's edge, she continued to listen and learned that someplace near Livingston Street was where they went. After that night, all she could think about was getting to Youngstown and seeing for herself.

⌘

Sarah knew there was a bus that went from Warren to Youngstown every day. People who lived in Warren but worked at the mill in Youngstown used it to get back and forth. She and her mother had taken it once to see Lucy's friend, Irma. Youngstown was a much bigger town compared to Warren. It even had one of those new department stores they advertised on the radio that people were talking about. It was less than an hour away, but it was a major event when anyone in her family got to go.

She got the schedule from the post office and found out the last bus left Warren at five thirty and arrived in Youngstown at six twenty. Sarah saved her money for the next two weeks to make the trip. She did every job she could think of. In addition to working at the pharmacy, she babysat Calvin, her neighbor Mrs. Lewis's bratty four-year-old son, and helped Miss Henry, who worked at the post office, dig and shovel dirt to clear the plot in her backyard for a summer garden. She even rode her bike a few mornings, delivering the *Tribune Chronicle* substituting for Tommy, the eleven-year-old down the street who came down with the measles. At the end of two weeks, she had three dollars and twenty-five cents and more than enough to cover the forty-five cent roundtrip ticket to Youngstown with money to spare.

Sarah's friend Rita was also on a quest to escape Warren. They had remained best friends all the way through school. Her dream was to move to Georgia, where her father lived. He and her mother had divorced two years earlier, and she missed him. Her mother's drinking, which led to their breakup, had gotten worse. She could become violent when she drank. After she slapped Rita across the face one night when she walked in the door only five minutes late for curfew, she said she couldn't take it anymore. Her father had written to her that there were lots of jobs in Savannah; she just needed to get there. So she agreed to come along on an expedition to Youngstown to find the place where girls made lots of money dancing in a show.

Sarah and Rita grew up more like sisters because their mothers were best friends. Both were the same age, but red-haired Rita was much more mature and practical. She was the reasonable one while carefree Sarah was prone to be spontaneous and foolish. Like the night their usual crowd from Saint Bernadette's were secretly at the creek down behind Blanton Farm, drinking homemade hooch and smoking cigarettes. It got late, and everybody was drunk but Rita, who didn't drink or smoke. The boys all chipped in whatever money they had and said they would give all of it to any girl who dared to go skinny-dipping in the creek.

"We got fifty cents here that says none of you girls will dare lose your clothes and jump in that creek!" Bill Sadler, intoxicated, yelled, pointing at the water.

When Sarah heard the dare and that there was money to be made, she wasted no time stripping down to her bare skin.

"No, don't do it, Sarah!" Rita screamed at her, as Sarah struggled to pull her green sweater over her head. Once again, she didn't listen and jumped in the cold water. About that time, Mr. Blanton heard the noise and showed up, shotgun in hand, and ran everybody off his property. In the dark, he didn't know there was a girl in the water until the rest of the group scattered, and he turned around and saw her.

"What are you doing, young lady? Get out of there and put your clothes on!" He swung his arm, motioning for her to get out of the water. Sarah emerged bent over at the waist, using her hands to cover her naked body. Mr. Blanton turned his back to give her some privacy. Shivering, she quickly put her clothes on over her wet skin.

"Don't ever let me catch you down here again, or I'll call the sheriff, you hear me?"

She stepped her damp feet into her shoes and ran off into the night as fast as she could. The incident was bad for Sarah's reputation. For weeks after, the boys and the girls, except for Rita, ignored her and could be heard whispering the word *slut* whenever she came around.

Embarrassed, she later confessed to Rita, "I should have listened to you."

Sarah was glad Sister Anne and Head Mother never heard about the gossip. She didn't want to think about the lecture they both would have given. Sister would have gotten angry and pointed her finger in her face while quoting Proverbs 28:26 for the hundredth time, "He who trust his own mind is a fool."

Head Mother would have told Brady and maybe even expelled her from school for behavior "unbecoming a Saint Bernadette young lady."

There were other times when Sarah's judgment was flawed. But Rita was always by her side, and somehow they remained friends through all of it. With more mistakes in her past than she cared to admit, Sarah realized she counted on Rita's level head.

When Friday came, Sarah told Brady she was spending the night at Rita's house, and Rita told her mother she would be at Sarah's. They were the first to get in line when they arrived at the bus stop next to the post office at five fifteen. A soothing velvet breeze was blowing air that was unusually warm for early spring. They ditched their jackets and wore the jazzy slim skirts and buttoned-up cardigans they bought while shopping in town together last month. The pale blue skirt and white sweater Sarah wore were complimented by a black clutch purse and shiny blue scarf she found in her mother's bureau. The scarf was around her neck and tied to one side the way she saw the New York models wearing. She also discovered a pair of black patent pumps in her mother's closet that looked like new and fit her perfectly. *I wonder if Mama ever got to wear these?* she thought when finding them.

Rather than her typical ponytail, Sarah let her sandy hair hang full and loose to her shoulders, which made her constantly have to swing her head back, trying to keep it out of her face. The scarlet lipstick she picked up at the pharmacy was bold and stylish. It was the same color the models were wearing. Looking fetching like she did, it would have been easy to mistake her for a young woman well into her twenties. Rita was in a pink skirt and blue sweater and had on plain black flats, her red hair pulled back into a single braid. Sarah, as usual, was the standout, but they were both fashionably attired and a noticeable contrast to the small-town simplicity of everyone else waiting for the bus.

One by one, people gathered in line behind them. The people coming from the mill were easily spotted. Men in their coveralls approached the line walking slowly, like they were exhausted from a long day, lunch pails in hand. By five thirty, about fifteen people were waiting for the bus that pulled up right on time. Sarah and Rita sat in the front two seats near the driver. The bus was old and worn. A few of the leather seats were patched with black tape to keep whatever stuffing was inside from escaping. And there was a detectable odor that was reminiscent of mildew and age. After everyone boarded, the driver closed the door, grabbed the huge steering wheel, and guided the bus from the curb out into the street. The girls looked at each other and giggled. At last, they were on their way. The driver, a colorless middle-aged man with heavy graying eyebrows and wire-rim glasses, had an honest face.

"Where you two pretty girls headed?" he asked as they got underway.

Sarah, still giggling, piped up, "We're on our way to be rich and famous!" She was bubbling with excitement.

Responding to her answer, he turned and looked over his shoulder.

"That's a lot to get done in a Friday evening." He sounded concerned.

Sarah smiled back but kept quiet, thinking it might not be smart to share too much about where they were going. As they neared Youngstown, Sarah leaned over from her seat and asked the driver which stop would put them near Livingston Street. The driver turned his head sharply to look at her.

"Livingston Street? Are you sure that's where you girls want to go? The colored folks live down there."

Rita squinted her eyes and frowned at Sarah. It was the first time she had heard that where they were going was in the colored part of town. Unlike Sarah and her family, she didn't really know anyone who wasn't white.

"Yes, we're sure. What stop should we take?" said Sarah.

"Suit yourself. I'll let you know when it's time to get off."

The gray bus gradually emptied as it made its way through several Youngstown neighborhoods. The longer they rode, the more the neighborhoods transitioned from those with middle-America manicured yards and freshly painted white picket fences, to older homes showing signs of neglect. Some had missing shutters and overdue repairs. Instead of mostly white people, like they saw at the first stop up on Main Street, they were seeing mainly colored people and only occasionally someone white.

"Your stop is coming up next."

They looked at each other, giggling. Their curiosity about the ladies who danced for lots of money was about to be satisfied.

"When is the last bus back to Warren tonight?" Sarah asked the driver.

"The last one picks up tonight at nine over on that corner." He nodded his head toward the opposite side of the street.

The bus began slowing down in preparation to stop. They stood up and smoothed down their skirts with their hands. Sarah, beginning to get nervous, ran her hands through her hair. Hastily, she took a small mirror from her purse and puckered her lips together and checked her appearance.

"You girls watch yourselves out there. Not a lot of white folk down here. I wouldn't want to see anything happen to you."

"We'll be careful," Sarah said, eager to get going.

When they came to a complete stop, Sarah asked the driver which way Livingston Street was.

"Walk down to the end of this street, and the cross street will be Livingston," he said, pointing.

"Okay, thank you."

They headed down the street in the direction he told them. When they reached the end of the block, there was no sign at the cross street, but they assumed it must have been Livingston, based on what the driver said. They looked to the right and the left, trying to decide which direction they should walk.

"Which way should we go?" Rita asked.

Just then, they saw three well-dressed Negro men on the opposite side of the street, heading south down Livingston.

"Let's follow them."

They crossed the street and began following them. The girls walked slow and kept at least a half-block distance behind them and the three men ahead so that they wouldn't be noticed. They walked briskly for some distance until they came to a corner with a small neighborhood bar. It had a sign that hung from a hook above the front door that said *Cousins*. The men looked long and hard in the window, as though trying to see if there was anyone inside they recognized. When they apparently didn't, they continued on their way. Sarah and Rita slowed their stride even more but never let them get too far out in front.

Out of nowhere, two Caucasian males came up from behind and startled the girls.

"You ought to be a shame! What the hell are two white girls doing down here on a Friday night?" the taller one shouted when they caught up with them and made moves to go around them on the street. The girls got nervous and didn't know what to say. They kept quiet and continued walking, their focus straight ahead, like they knew where they were going. As the two men passed, Sarah managed a quick look at their faces. She wasn't positive, but she thought she remembered seeing the shorter one at one of the Saturday-night parties at their house.

As they moved on, the one who had spoken kept walking but looked back at them over his shoulder. "You should go home! This neighborhood is no place for white girls!" he yelled back at them and then went on their way.

Sarah felt a queasy knot rise in her stomach. It was like the feeling she got at school when Sister Anne would ask her to stand and read the English lesson to the class. She was a good reader, but nervous insecurity consumed her when having to do it in front of the class.

She began to question if this expedition had been a good idea or not.

What would Sister Anne say if she knew what we were doing? Probably quote Proverbs 28:26.

Everything Sarah heard in her head and sensed inside herself screamed of Sister Anne's disappointment. But her stubborn determination ruled, and she convinced herself that this was something she had to do.

God, please keep us safe.

"What have you gotten me into now, Sarah?" said Rita.

She grabbed Rita's hand tight, and the two continued walking.

They slowed down more and allowed a wide distance to separate them from the two men ahead and the belittling comments the tall one made. They came to the top of a hill. The three Negro men they were following earlier had completely disappeared from sight. The sun was going down, and the changing illumination was bouncing off the tin roofs of the tight rows of houses that lined both sides of the street.

The further they walked, the more the appearance of the neighborhood grew grim. The houses were becoming more and more neglected, many of them overdue for a paint job, and some even with abandoned cars and unguarded furniture in the yards. Their surroundings felt desperate. They looked and felt out of place. The occasional person they passed on the street stared at them. An older colored woman, with a black eye, approached and asked them for money. She was wearing an old gray dress that was torn a little at the shoulder. It was dirty. When they passed her, the distinct scent of urine caught Sarah's nostrils. When she told her they didn't have any money, she got angry and shouted, "Cracker white girls. Y'all ain't got no business down here no way. Must be headed to *520* with your low-down selves."

After a while, the two white men they were following slowed their pace and eventually stopped in front of a large Victorian house. It was very well kept, with a fresh coat of light-green paint and a well-landscaped yard. Its size and well-appointed features made it distinct from the other dilapidated houses on the street. It stood like an oasis in an otherwise desolate community. The men opened the metal gate and closed it behind them. They made their way up the short sidewalk and onto the wide porch that wrapped around the front. A green-and-white metal awning hung low and covered the porch. Smaller matching awnings were at each of the five front windows.

"Something is going on at that house," Sarah said as she quickened her steps.

"Sarah, I don't know about this." Rita came to a dead stop and looked at her.

"What's going on at that house might not be what we thought. Maybe we should just go on back home," she said with a worried look.

"I didn't come all this way to turn around and go home without finding out how those girls are making money." Sarah was agitated.

"All right, but I'm getting a bad feeling about this."

"Think about this as an adventure. Nothing this exciting ever happens in Warren, and you know it! Let's just find out what's going on in that house. If it's different than we thought or we don't like it, we'll just go home, okay?"

"All right," Rita replied, reluctant.

They headed down the hill, holding hands and focusing on the big house. As they got closer, they saw the number *520* prominently painted in white on the awning over the porch steps. When they reached the gate, they looked at each other. Sarah took a deep breath, summoned her courage, and opened the gate. The two walked into the yard and up the walk to the porch. Climbing the steps, they could see two men were standing at the front door. Both were over-sized with bulky chests and biceps that poked through the jackets of their black suits. The biggest one of the two was raven and the other, snowy-pale. They looked distinguished but intimidating. Rita punched Sarah with her elbow when she saw them as they neared the top of the steps. When they stepped onto the porch, the pale one moved forward to meet them.

"Can we help you, ladies?"

"Ughh, we're looking for jobs," Sarah said, trying to sound grown-up. "My uncle told me girls make good money here."

He looked back at his partner and grinned.

"We do hire girls here. If you're looking for jobs, I'll go get the boss."

"Yes, can we talk to him?" She was nervously excited.

"Sure, wait here. I'll see if I can get him." He opened one side of the big double front doors and went inside.

The dark man that remained closed the door and resumed his post in front of it. The girls stood there awkwardly, not knowing whether to strike up a conversation or just stay quiet and wait. After a minute or so, Rita took a few steps back from the door and pulled on Sarah's arm to do the same.

"I'm nervous about this," she said, pressing her shoulder into Sarah's and whispering.

"Don't be nervous." She took Rita's hand and got close in her face. "I told you, if it's different from what we thought, we'll just leave, okay? But we can't come all this way and not know what's going on in there."

"Okay, but promise me we'll leave if we don't like it," Rita said, timid.

"I promise!" Her response was sharp and had an annoyed edge.

The door opened, and a muscular, caramel-colored Negro man walked out onto the porch. Likely in his midthirties, he wore a well-fitted silver-gray suit, his hair black, sharply styled and shining. A thick black mustache complimented the sharp contours of his face. He held his body strong and confident when he came through the door.

Sarah and Rita were stunned when seeing him and spontaneously both inhaled. His Thurgood Marshall looks and broad stature overwhelmed them. He was unlike anyone the two unsuspecting country girls from Warren had ever seen.

As he came toward them, Sarah noticed that his eyes were hazel. Never had she seen a colored man with hazel eyes. When he reached where they were, he assumed a broad, solid stance with his hands crossed at the wrist in front of his body. The diamond rings he wore on both pinky fingers twinkled and added a stylish class to a commanding presence.

"Good evening, ladies. My name is Wallace. Can I help you?" His tenor voice was strong and authoritative. There was a sparkle from a gold tooth in the top right front of his mouth when he spoke.

"Ahh, yes, sirr," Sarah said, slurring. "We heard girls can get jobs here that pay well."

"We do hire pretty girls here. Did somebody send you?" He looked at them bizarrely.

"I heard my uncle and his friends talk about this place, so we came to see for ourselves."

"This is a place for grown folks. Are you two old enough to be here?" he joked, but was clearly waiting on their response.

"Yes sir, we're old enough." Rita let Sarah do all the talking.

"Well, come on in. I'll show you around."

He held out his hand for Sarah to take. She turned and looked at Rita, uncertain, then grinned and gave him her hand. He pulled it toward his bicep so that she would take hold of it. Grabbing his big taut arm, Sarah got a whiff of him. His scent was intoxicating—a manly combination of musk and lavender. His scent made her feel strangely disoriented. A rush of energy flowed down from her head and came to rest in the pit of her stomach. She had never felt anything like it before.

He's so handsome! And a grown man…maybe even a rich one! He was more than she could imagine.

She took a moment and looked again over her shoulder to make sure Rita was still there and then turned back and looked up at him. All she could think was that he was the most handsome man she had ever seen, and like a princess, she was holding his strong arm and being escorted inside. Rita followed close behind as they stepped inside the front door.

Chapter 4

The door closed behind them, and they found themselves standing on the landing of a grand foyer. The stateliness of the place was unlike anything they had seen before. To the right was a huge parlor. In it were several people sitting around at tables, drinking and talking. A small bar with a bartender was near the rear of the room. The lighting was dim and colored by red. To their left was a registration desk, like the one you would see at a hotel. A matronly dressed colored lady with silver-gray hair and the wrinkling face of a grandmother sat behind it, reading the newspaper. She glanced up over her glasses when they entered but wasted no time getting back to her reading. Standing there on the landing, with three steps down to a foyer, they had a full view of the wide-open area. It was accentuated by a wide red-carpeted staircase that led up to the second floor. An open circular hallway on the upper level spanned out in both directions from the stairs.

"What do you girls drink?" Wallace asked. They followed him back toward the bar.

Rita looked at Sarah, unsure. As Wallace walked ahead, Sarah put her index finger to her lips, signaling for Rita to be quiet.

"We both drink whiskey," Sarah said.

She had never had a drink of whiskey but remembered that Brady seemed to always reach for a bottle of it whenever his friends came by the house.

"Three whiskeys," Wallace said to the Negro man behind the counter when they approached the bar.

"You girls came on a good night. Friday is one of our busiest, but it's early yet. By eleven, this whole downstairs will be jumping with music and dancing. Maybe you can stick around."

"Oh, we love to dance!" Sarah grinned and giggled.

"I like your dimple." Wallace put a light hand to her cheek, admiring it. Sarah felt weak when he touched her. "The customers would love that."

The bartender put three small glasses containing a brown liquid down in front of them. Nervously, the girls each took one and raised the glasses to their lips. Taking a sip, they tried not to choke.

"So what brings you young ladies here tonight?" asked Wallace. He took a huge gulp of his drink.

Sarah, eager as always, spoke up and said, "We have big plans, but we need money. We heard the pay is good here."

Wallace gazed at them, puzzled, and arched one eye. "So you want to make some money? Exactly what do you think girls do here to make all that money?"

"That's what we came here to find out," she said.

"My guess is they're dancers and entertain the customers. Is that right?" Sarah looked up at him with the curiosity of a child. "I overheard my uncle say one of the girls was really good."

"Well, I guess you could say they're entertainers," he joked. "It's their job to make sure the male guests have a good time when they come here." He was friendly, but his tone shifted, and he became more businesslike and serious.

"How do they do that?" asked Rita without a clue.

He changed the subject. "Just how old are you girls?"

They turned and looked at each other as though trying to decide on the right answer. Obviously, seventeen would have been too young to be there. Sarah winked her eye at Rita while her back was toward Wallace, then she turned to him.

"We're both twenty-two."

"Twenty-two is good. What are your names?"

"I'm Sarah, and this is Rita."

"Well, Sarah and Rita, if you really want to know how girls make money here, I can show you much better than I can tell you. Would you like a tour?"

"Yes!" Sarah was excited by the idea.

"Well, finish your drinks, and I'll show you around." While he waited for them to finish their whiskey, Wallace looked with intention around the room like he was patrolling it.

Anxious to take the tour, they held their breaths and drank their drinks as fast as they could. When Rita finally sat her glass down on the bar, she swayed backward a bit. Catching herself, she looked at Sarah.

"Oh my goodness, I'm really dizzy," she said quietly.

"It's just the drink." Sarah, trying to sound experienced, wouldn't admit that her head was spinning too.

"Come on, ladies, let me show you how grown folks have fun."

Wallace leaned his head back, emptied his glass, slammed it down on the bar, then led them back out into the foyer and over to the registration desk. The woman behind the desk was still reading the paper.

"Miss Betty, I'd like you to meet Sarah and Rita."

She looked up from her paper and peered over her reading glasses at them.

"What we got here, Wallace?" she asked him gruffly.

"These ladies want to know how girls make money here."

Miss Betty chuckled under her breath in a mocking tone. When she did, it reminded Sarah of the time she got caught behind the school with Robert Perry by Sister Martha. On a dare, she had let him put his hand under her skirt. When Sister found them, she yelled, "Sarah!" with such outrage.

After she pulled her skirt down and pushed Robert away, she heard Sister make the same judgmental sound Miss Betty just had.

"Miss Betty is really the one who runs this place, girls. You need anything, just see her. Let me take you upstairs." Wallace motioned for them to follow him.

"Which one is occupied, Miss Betty?" he asked, looking over his shoulder at her as he headed toward the staircase.

"Number four," she said.

"Okay, perfect."

Sarah and Rita followed Wallace up the staircase. When they reached the top step, they were face-to-face with a huge grandfather clock. It was the centerpiece of the two hallways. Its dark wood cabinet housed a huge gold pendulum. It was an impressive piece of furniture and must have stood at least six feet. As they walked passed it, they both took note of the time. They looked at each other but didn't speak. It was nearing eight o'clock.

They followed Wallace down the hall to a closed wooden door with a small sign that read *Office*. He opened it with his key, and they all went inside. It was a spacious room furnished with a mahogany desk and two comfortable chairs positioned in front of it. A couch with the same brown leather as the chairs was against the wall behind them. Wallace sat down in the high-back chair behind the desk and motioned for them to sit.

"Okay, ladies, here's the story. The girls that work here make a lot of money because they pleasure men. Whatever a man wants, they know they can come here, and these girls will make sure they have a good time."

"They pleasure men! Do you mean like sex?" Rita asked in her usual naive way.

"Yes, if that's what the customer wants. But this is a very professionally run establishment. We take care of our girls. Nothing trashy happening here."

"Do the girls here really go all the way?" Rita said, her eyes as wide as they could get.

"Like I said earlier, I can show you better than I can tell you."

Wallace turned off the lamp on the desk, putting them in total darkness. He moved his chair to one side and opened a small sliding door in the wall. There was a glass panel in the opening, and it looked right into the next room. As the girls leaned to the edge of their chairs to see, they got a glimpse of a naked man and woman on a bed in the next room. The woman was on top of the man straddling him and had what looked like a horsewhip in her right hand. She moved as if trying to stay straddled to a wild bull while keeping the whip in motion, circling it above her head. The man appeared to keep her steady by holding both her breasts in each hand. Wallace let them look for a few seconds and then closed the sliding door. He turned on the light and moved his chair back to its original position. The girls fell back hard in their chairs, breathless and shocked by what they had just seen.

"Ladies, that's what girls do here for money."

For the first time since they arrived, Sarah had nothing to say. Rita, on the other hand, became frantic.

"Oh my goodness! Sarah, did you see that? These women are having sex with these men!"

"Yes, I saw," she told her in an eerily calm voice.

"So how much will that lady make tonight?" Sarah asked Wallace in a direct, nearly unshaken voice.

"Before the night ends, she will probably have made about ten dollars."

"Ten dollars! Really! Are you hiring?"

"Sarah!" Rita shrieked. "Do you know what you're saying? These women are doing awful things here!"

"What I know, Rita, is there is nowhere in Warren we can make ten dollars in one night!"

Sarah sounded strangely unlike herself. If she could make that much cash in one night, she calculated in her head how quickly she could have the money she needed to get a bus ticket to New York plus enough to get settled once she got there.

This job would just be temporary until I can make what I need, and then I'll quit and leave, she thought.

Wallace looked at her, surprised by the conviction in her response.

"Yes, I'm hiring. I'm always in the market for a pretty girl," he said flirtatiously. "You think you wanna work here?"

"Yes, sir, I do! When can I start?"

Chapter 5

They missed the 9:00 p.m. bus back to Warren, so Wallace drove them home, just as the sun was coming up. They were exhausted. It was the first time either of them had stayed up all night. And what a night it had been...

After he showed Sarah and Rita how the girls at *520* made their livings, Wallace proceeded to take them on a tour of the rest of the house. When they exited the office, he turned and locked the door with his key. Standing there in the hallway waiting for him, they had a chance to gaze long around the open balcony of the second floor. It was grand, like a mansion. Downstairs, they could see more people had arrived—mostly men—and swing music was playing in the background on the Victrola. There were six doors on the upper level—three to the right of the stairs and three more on the left. After the horrifying sight they just witnessed through the panel in the office, Sarah's imagination ran wild with images of what might be taking place behind those closed doors. Perhaps in the first, there was a man and woman kissing and laughing while sipping champagne. In the second, maybe there was another naked couple like the one they just saw in the office, but this time, the man was on top and the woman was below. That was the position she heard and assumed sex always took place in and not like what she saw. She knew nothing about sexual relations and wondered how she would ever learn. She began second-guessing her earlier reaction and whether or not Rita had been right—that they really should have turned around and gone home. And now that the big mystery was solved, why were they still there? She felt a rush inside that made her light-headed. Suddenly, all of it was more than the experience of her seventeen years could handle, and she was spinning.

After locking the door, Wallace led them down the hall to the right. Rita hadn't said a word since her frantic outburst in the office. Sarah knew her friend and could sense how tense and scared she was. If she agreed to work there, Rita would not come with her. She would be totally on her own. The thought of not having Rita alongside as a trusted security blanket pulled at her stomach. Despite all that, she was still excited at the thought of having found a place where she could make lots of money, and fast.

If things work out, I can have enough money to be on my way to New York by August. Her mind was busy planning and calculating as she walked behind Wallace down the hall.

I can help Uncle Brady with the bills too. Uncle Brady!

In an instant, she could see his face.

I can never tell him this is where I work.

Wallace guided them around the hallway and along the open banister. The door of each room had a black number on it. When they got to number six, the last door, he stopped and tapped soft on it three times.

"Shirley," he said, in a voice that was sultry but delivered with authority. "It's WB, open the door."

Within a few seconds, the door cracked, and over Wallace's huge shoulders, Sarah caught a glimpse of a petite young ebony girl. She didn't look much older than her and Rita. She was naturally attractive with long black hair that was straight like a white girl's. When she appeared in the doorway, Wallace relaxed his body and leaned against the frame.

"Hey, Miss Shirley," he whispered.

Is that his girlfriend? Sarah thought.

She surprised herself by feeling a little jealous that Wallace might have a girlfriend.

Why should I care? We just met him. She wrinkled her face in a frown, confused at the thought.

"I got two new girls here I want you to talk to. Let 'em know how things run around here. You know, show 'em the ropes. Can you do that for WB?" he said, licking his lips and smiling.

"Sure, baby," she responded.

Wallace stepped aside so they could all see each other.

"Shirley, this is Sarah, and… I'm sorry, sweetheart, I forgot your name."

"It's Rita," she said, annoyed.

"Yeah, that's right, Sarah and Rita. Ladies, this is Shirley. She can tell you everything about *520* you need to know. Right, Shirley?" She didn't speak but pretended to smile at them.

"Well, ladies, I've gotta get back to work, so I will leave you two with Shirley.

He looked at Shirley with an odd eye that seemed to communicate additional meanings that she apparently understood.

"Ladies, you couldn't be in better hands than with Shirley here. Take your time and get to know each other. I'll check in on you later."

He ushered them in the direction of the open door to Shirley's room and then took off down the hall.

"Y'all come on in," Shirley said, motioning with her hand.

Sarah grabbed Rita's hand to try to reassure her. They walked into Shirley's room, and she closed the door.

The small but tidy bedroom was decorated with more tones of red, just like much of the rest of the house but also black. The bed appeared freshly made and was covered by a shiny red spread that glistened in the light of the lamp that was on the table sitting next to it. Across the bed was a small velvet settee couch with fluffy black pillows and a red armchair near it. The girls sat down nervously on the couch. Shirley walked barefooted toward the chair as she tried to hold together the front of the short pink robe she was wearing. It was easy to see that she had little on under it. When she sat down, she crossed her bare mahogany legs at the knee, took a cigarette from the case on the table, lit it, and took a deep drag. She exhaled a big puff of smoke and blew it in their faces, then leaned in and looked at them.

"Okay, so what the hell are you two dewy-eyed white girls doing here? You don't look like you're supposed to be here. Do you even know what goes on in this place?"

The questions Shirley fired at them were simple and direct, but no answers followed. Neither knew what to say.

"We don't get a lot of white girls here. Y'all should probably be talking to Loretta."

"Who's Loretta?" Sarah asked.

"She's a white girl that works here. The men like her. You'll meet her. She's older and been here a lot longer than me."

"Do you live here?" Sarah asked.

"Not all the time. Most everybody is just here on the weekends. 520 is open for business evenings from Thursday to Saturday. We usually finish up around 3:00 a.m. I come in on Friday night after I finish my other job. During the week, me and my mama clean houses and do laundry on the other side of town." Shirley held her cigarette ladylike between two fingers and took another drag.

"Does your mama know you work here?" Sarah was thinking of Brady and what he might do if he found out she had a job there.

"Yeah, my mama knows!" she responded sharply. "She also knows it's just me, her, and my little brothers, and if I didn't work here, we can't pay the rent. I ain't proud of it, but I'm doing what I have to do to keep a roof over our heads."

"Why are you here?" Shirley quickly changed the subject and looked directly at Sarah.

"Well, I need money so I can move to New York by the end of the summer."

"What's in New York?"

"I don't know, but I want to find out."

Shirley laughed. "That sounds like some kinda stupid dream."

"What about you? What's your story, Red?" Referring to her hair, Shirley shifted to Rita.

"I just came here with Sarah. I won't be working here." Rita's response was quick and full of disdain.

"Sounds to me like neither one of y'all need to be here." She looked at Sarah. "Have you ever been with a man before? Because you look green as hell!" It wasn't funny, but Shirley laughed.

"No, but I could learn. How did you learn?"

"I learned the hard way with one of my mama's boyfriends. That's how I learned!" she came back at her hard. "I wouldn't recommend that way to nobody."

Shirley paused for a second, and her eyes filled as she appeared to be remembering something dark from her past.

"WB teaches girls that don't know."

"You mean Wallace?"

"Yeah, we all call him WB. He looks out for us. We don't have no cause to worry about any of these fools trying to take advantage or get rough. They know WB and his boys don't put up with no foolishness. One night, a man got drunk and tried to rough up one of the other girls. WB's men beat him up real bad and then threw him out in the street."

They stayed in Shirley's room talking for a long time. Sarah found out a full session with a customer is an hour long and cost four dollars. Girls get two dollars of that, and the other half goes to the house. Miss Betty has a menu the men select from. Sunday morning at breakfast, everyone gets paid. Miss Betty takes care of the girls, making sure they have soap, towels, and sheets, along with a supply of the prophylactics they were required to use.

"The worst thing that can happen is for a girl to get pregnant, so you better use the rubbers. This one girl, Anna, got pregnant last year. She tried to hide it for a long time, but when WB found out, he went off on her! Never seen him that mad before. She had a baby right here in the house one night. I can still hear her screaming for her son. Miss Betty took it away as soon as it was born, but nobody knew where. Anna never seen her baby again."

Sarah's eyes were wide as she listened. "Did she keep working here after they took her baby?"

"She tried to for a while, but she was so sad on account of losing her child. Men didn't want to be with her no more. Said she wasn't no fun no more. WB finally told her she had to leave."

When Shirley finished the story, they all kept quiet, as if they were all paying a moment of silence to Anna and the baby she lost.

Just then, the music downstairs got louder. Shirley started moving her hips in the chair to the sound of it.

"Oh yeah! The party is starting! If y'all don't have no mo' questions, I need to get to work and make some money. Why don't you go downstairs and have a drink?"

Shirley got up from her chair and made a few steps in the direction of the door to let them know it was time for them to leave.

"I'll see you all the time if you come work here," she told Sarah.

"All right, thanks for talking to us." She and Rita got up slow and seemingly unsure of what they were to do next.

Shirley walked them to the door. When she opened it, the music from downstairs rushed in. They walked over to the rail and could see that the foyer and the bar were bustling. At the bottom of the stairs in the open foyer, a few couples were dancing to Cab Calloway. Shirley leaned over the rail and waved her hand to get the attention of Miss Betty, who was still at the desk. When they locked eyes, Shirley raised the index finger of her right hand, and Betty nodded back at her.

"Okay, I'll see you two later. I gotta get to work."

Shirley gave Sarah a guarded smile and went back into her room and closed the door.

"I guess we should go downstairs," Sarah said, looking at Rita.

"What we should do is get out of this place! What time is it anyway?"

Both remembered the clock at the top of the stairs and walked toward it. It was almost 10:00 p.m.

"Oh, my! How did it get so late! We've missed the bus back to Warren. How are we supposed to get home?" Rita was desperate.

"We'll figure something out, don't worry. Let's just go downstairs. Maybe we can find somebody that will give us a ride."

"We should have left earlier! I knew when we came out of that office, this was no place for us." Rita stood firm and folded her arms. She had had enough.

Knowing there was nothing she could say to make her feel better, Sarah began slowly walking down the stairs toward the people below. Mad and sulking, Rita followed behind her, sluggish.

The crowd was alive with men and women swing dancing and having a good time. Most of the men wore dark suits with white shirts and ties and topped off by dark-colored fedora hats. The ladies had on brightly colored dresses with skirts that moved as they danced. On her way down the stairs, Sarah ran into a man on his way up. Recognizing his crew cut hair, she knew he was the same one that had harassed her and Ruth on the street earlier that evening.

"Well, well, well, we meet again," he said.

"I knew this was where you two were headed."

He spoke to her in the same condescending tone he had on the street. But he kept going up the steps like he was in a hurry to get someplace. When he passed Rita, he looked at her with the same contempt. Sarah slowed her decline and looked over her head to follow him. He walked down the hallway to Shirley's room and knocked on the door. When the door opened, Sarah could see Shirley's pink robe and her bare legs. She greeted him with a smile, grabbed his hand, pulled him inside, and shut the door.

Sarah made her descent into the haze of cigarette smoke that had settled on the crowd. Rita followed close, and they both submerged into the mix of people moving about.

Sarah made her way back to the bar. The bartender that had served them whiskey earlier that evening was busy pouring drinks. He moved as fast as he could, trying to keep up with all the drink requests from the people standing around the bar. He poured, shook, and served with the speed and accuracy of a pro.

"Yes, ma'am, what can I get you?" he asked Sarah after he had the rush under control.

"Oh, I don't want anything."

"You sure 'bout that? 'Cause if you don't want nothing to drink, you need to move away from the bar and make room for paying customers."

Sarah thought for a second. The room was packed with faces of people she and Rita had never seen. At least there at the bar, the bartender would know they came in with Wallace.

"Okay, ughh, do you have ginger ale?"

He looked at her, and his eyes widened. "Folks don't much order that, but I think I can find some. You waiting for the boss?"

"Yes, is he still here?"

"I saw him a while ago. Not sure where he is now, but he'll be back through here before long. My name is Sam." His smile was pleasant.

"Mine is Sarah."

"Nice to meet you, Miss Sarah. I'll get you that ginger ale."

Sam was probably in his forties. He had a noticeable limp, though it didn't seem to slow him down much. He went about fixing drinks and wobbling from one end of the bar to the other. Sarah figured something must have had happened to him in the war to make him walk like that. Sarah thought he seemed nice, so staying near him by the bar felt like a safe place to anchor until they could find a way home.

Just when Sam returned with the glass of ginger ale, Rita emerged out of the crowd.

"Where were you?" Sarah asked her.

"I went out back to pee."

"I should probably do that too," she told her. "Are you still mad?"

"I just want to go home." Rita's voice was empty.

While the girls waited by the bar, a graying man staggered up to them. He was drunk, and his belly hung low over his belted waist. The suit jacket he was attempting to look sporting in fit him tight around the shoulders and was at least two sizes too small.

"Lordie, what we got here!" he said, looking at the two of them.

"Two white beauties, just ripe for the picking!"

At about the same time, Wallace appeared out of nowhere. "Floyd, you need to move it along. These ladies don't work for the house."

"Ohhh, no problem, Wallace. You know I don't want no trouble."

He licked his lips and took a final lustful look at them, then moved on into the shuffle of people.

"So how you girls doing? Did you get to know Shirley? Did she answer all your questions?"

Wallace was as curious as he was handsome. The music blared while Sarah thought carefully about her response.

"Yes, I think we got all the answers to our questions." She looked up at him, his broad body hovering over her.

"Okay, good. Think you still wanna work here?"

Knowing that Rita was completely opposed to everything they had seen and heard, Sarah didn't want her to hear her response to Wallace's question. She leaned in his direction to speak quietly in his ear. When she did, she was deliciously overpowered by the scent of his cologne.

"Can I talk to you in private? My friend is not comfortable. But I still have a few more questions."

"Of course."

"Sam!" Wallace motioned to him with his hand and he immediately came over to see what he needed.

"Sam, can you keep an eye on Miss Rita here for a few minutes?"

"No problem, boss."

"Give her whatever she wants."

"Rita, I'll be back in a few minutes, I promise," Sarah said.

"All right, but don't break your promise like you did before," Rita said, still resentful about the broken promise Sarah made earlier that they would leave if this place wasn't what they thought.

"I promise."

Wallace led her around the corner of the bar to a darkened narrow hallway that took them toward the back of the house. As she followed him away from the crowd of people, she grew anxious at the thought of being alone with him. The further they moved away from the noise, the more the creak of the old wood floor was noticeable under their feet. Wallace walked to the end of the hall and opened a door on the left. He stood to the side after he opened it and gentlemanly allowed her to enter ahead of him. It was a small storage room stocked tightly with supplies for the house. There were sheets and towels all folded neatly on shelves that reached toward the low-hanging ceiling. On one side, there were shelves filled with drinking glasses arranged by size and lined up together. The cramped space smelled stale with age. In the small cleared area near the door, a single light bulb hung from the ceiling on a chain. It was on when they entered but provided only a dim illumination of the contents in the room.

Wallace closed the door, and they stood facing each other with the light hanging just above his head. Sarah felt small standing so close to him. She always thought of herself as tall, but the top of her head was level to his broad chest. Looking up at him, she could see that the hazel in his eyes also had hints of green and brown, which the light made more noticeable.

"So what did you wanna tell me that you couldn't say in front of your friend?"

"I was wondering if you would let me try working here? Sort of like a test to see if I was any good or not." She sounded naive and unsure.

"A test, huh?"

"Shirley told me a lot, but there is still a lot I would need to learn."

"Are you trying to say you're a virgin?" Wallace's brow wrinkled.

Sarah dropped her head down and away, embarrassed by the question and not wanting to look at him when she gave her answer.

"Yes."

"Look at me." He put his hand to her chin and raised it toward him.

"You don't have no reason to be embarrassed." He was direct and caring. "Why did you come here tonight, Sarah? You seem like a girl from a good family. Most of the girls working here came on hard times and needed to make some money just to survive. That's not your story, is it?"

"No, I guess not," she said, low and feeling silly like she had been exposed.

"I'm just sick of boring Warren. I feel like if I don't get out of there, I'm going to die. My mama tried to get out, but she couldn't because she didn't have any money. And there was nobody to help her. She died not knowing what her life could have been. I'm determined not to let that happen to me. I need to escape for me and for her. I figure if I work here for a little while, I can make some fast money. My plan is to move to New York in a few months." She gushed with amplified emotion as she told him about her plans.

"Okay, well, I can teach you everything you need to know. Besides, a lot of these men come here not as much interested in having sex as they just want to spend time with a pretty girl."

"You mean I could work here and not have to have sex with anybody!" She got excited.

"No, I'm not saying that. What I am saying is that if you want to work here, I can teach you how to be one of the girls, and that does include sex. But if you want to start slow, you can do that until I think you're ready. Sort of like a 'test.'" He smiled and used air quotes to make fun of her earlier use of the word.

"You're a beautiful dame. You could be one of the most popular girls here. Listen, I'll take care of you. You can best believe I'll make sure nobody hurts you. You gotta trust me, though, and do what I tell you. If you think you can do that, then we got a deal."

He held his hand out for her to shake it and finalize their agreement. Sarah looked at his big hand for a moment and contemplated if she should take it. Knowing if she did, there was no turning back. Then she thought about how her life would finally be interesting.

With the money I'll be making, this could be the beginning of everything I've wanted my whole life! Plus I would get to be around him all the time. The thought of seeing him regularly was all the bonus she needed.

Sarah looked up at him, grabbed his hand, and shook it. When she did, he seized the opportunity and, powerful but gentle, pulled her body into his. Before she realized what was happening, he leaned down and kissed her on the lips. It was soft like the cozy feeling of being under the covers on a winter morning. She felt his breath on her face. The smell of whiskey and Aqua Velva combined perfectly and stimulated her. When his tongue touched hers, she thought she might faint. The feeling that welled up from her stomach was over-powering, unlike anything she had ever experienced.

Wallace pulled away but remained fixed on her. The furrow in his brow created an expression on his face that indicated the unexpected had just happened. Sarah kept her eyes closed, and her lips puckered for a few seconds longer with her head still tilted up toward him like she was in a foggy trance.

"Do you have a way to get home?"

His tone was changed. It was softer, almost vulnerable.

"No," she said, shaken and trying not to appear rattled.

"If you can wait a while, I can drive you and your friend back to Warren."

"All right. Thank you."

Chapter 6

It was five thirty Saturday morning when they got to Warren. Wallace's blue Buick was one of only a few cars on the road at that hour. He had them both sit in the back seat to give the appearance that he was their chauffeur in case they were stopped by the police or anyone else, for that matter, who might be curious why a colored man had two white girls in his car. Rita fell asleep as soon as they got on the road.

⌒∾⌒

When Sarah returned to the bar from the storage room, Rita was in the same spot and keeping company with Sam while he poured drinks and waited on customers. They were laughing and talking with each other. When she approached to join them, Rita barely acknowledged her presence. Sarah stood there for a while, but when there didn't seem to be any attempt to include her in the conversation, she began feeling ignored. Seeing that one of the small tables in the corner was empty, she decided to take it. She spent the rest of the evening sitting alone, people watching, waiting for Wallace. From where she sat, she had full view of the front desk and was able to observe how gray-haired Miss Betty managed everything that went on upstairs.

When a male customer approached the desk, she peered at him over reading glasses that were connected to a black cord that hung around her neck. Whatever information it was she exchanged with them, she wrote down in a black leather book. Afterward, they handed her money, which she put in a gray strongbox she kept under the desk.

After about an hour, the man she had earlier sent up to Shirley's room came down the stairs, stepping like a peacock. He adjusted his tie with both hands and grinned a satisfied grin, similar to the way one would look after having enjoyed a good meal. Sarah saw two other girls emerge from their rooms at different times and give Miss Betty the same index finger signal like Shirley had done. Soon afterward, she watched one man and then another make their way up the stairs, knock on a girl's door, and get pulled inside. There was also a young colored boy, who couldn't have been more than fifteen, that worked there. He wore a white shirt with red suspenders attached to black trousers that came up short on his ankles. After each man left a girl's room, he carried white folded sheets and towels up to them. Miss Betty spoke at him and pointed her finger in various directions, obviously giving him instructions on what to do. Finishing his deliveries, he returned to the desk and took a seat on a stool behind her chair and waited for her to tell him what to do next. Sarah observed that there was a system to all that went on there.

While waiting for Wallace, she had a hard time fending off the men who kept approaching her. One middle-aged man, wearing wired glasses and looking a little like Brady, asked her if she was one of the "sportin' girls." At first, she didn't quite know what he meant but quickly figured out that was the name the men gave the girls that worked upstairs. Sarah ignored him and didn't answer but thought to herself, *I'll be a sporting girl?*

As hard as she tried to stay awake and keep Wallace company on the drive home, she fell asleep in the back next to Rita. As they got close to Warren, he put his hand over the seat and touched her leg. She immediately woke up.

"You'll need to show me how to get to your house," he said.

"Oh, okay," she responded, dazed.

"Would you mind dropping Rita at her house first?"

"No problem. Just show me which way to go."

Sarah was thinking it might be better if Rita got out first; that way, she wouldn't hear her conversation with Wallace about *520* and when she would start work there.

"Two blocks down, you'll make a right," she told him. "Rita, we're almost at your house," Sarah said, shaking her on the leg.

Rita woke up groggy and confused but didn't say anything as she rubbed at her eyes. By the time Wallace made the turn onto her street, she was fully awake and sitting straight up like she couldn't wait to get out of the car.

"It's the house with the green awnings up on the right," Sarah told him.

Wallace steered the car to the curb in front of Rita's house.

"Here you go, Miss Rita. I hope you had a good time tonight."

"Thank you, Wallace. See you later, Sarah."

Rita's face and voice were void of expression as she quickly got out of the car and closed the door. Sarah sank inside, worried their friendship was about to change because of the choice she was making. Rita was her best friend. But just like always, Sarah was being the risk-taker while Rita played it safe. She watched through the back seat window as Rita walked up the concrete steps to her front porch, put the key in the door, and went inside.

"Where to now?" Wallace asked. He was completely unaware of the fracture that had just taken place between two longtime friends.

"If you take a left, my house is about a half mile down on the right."

Brady was on her mind and whether or not he would be home. Sometimes on Friday nights, if he drank too much, he stayed at Claude's and didn't come home until Saturday afternoon. She was hoping that would be the case and she would make it home before he did. Digging in her purse for the door key, she considered what she would say to him if he were home.

"So when will I see you again, Sarah?"

After he turned the corner, Wallace slowed the car down and took his time getting to her house.

"You can start work anytime you like. Just let me know when."

"Well, I was thinking I could work the same schedule Shirley does, Friday to Sunday," she said timidly from the back seat. "Only thing is, I can ride the bus to get there, but I don't have a way to get back to Warren, like tonight."

"Not a problem. Now that I know where you live, I can introduce you to my girl Loretta. She lives in Warren too and not that far from here. She's older than you, but she's the other white girl that works at the house. Loretta has a car and drives to Youngstown. Between the two of us, we should be able to get you home."

Sarah remembered Shirley talking about Loretta as the white girl that worked there.

"As pretty as you are, you're gon' make us a lot of money, so I'll do whatever to make this work."

"All right, so what if I start next Friday night?"

"Sounds like a winner," he said.

"The gray one up on your right is my house," she told him as they got closer.

She could see Brady's dirt-caked red pickup in the front yard. Her stomach tightened. She was embarrassed for Wallace to see their house and how unkempt it was. It needed painting. One of the window shutters was still detached and hanging down following a storm over a year ago. It was one of many things Brady never seemed to get around to fixing. No one would ever guess a handyman lived there. What once was a nice flower bed along the walk up to the front porch, and the pride of her mother, had become a gathering place for overgrown weeds. After the evening she spent in the luxury of *520*, she was more aware than ever of the neglected condition of their house.

"Okay, well I guess this is it," she said, as Wallace brought the car to a stop.

He turned around and looked back at her from the front seat. "Nice to meet you, Sarah. I'll look forward to seeing you again and you being part of our little family. So I guess I'll see you on Friday, right?"

"Okay, what time should I get there?"

"Why don't you make it around seven o'clock? That will give me time to do some training with you before customers start showing up. Gotta get you ready to pass the test." He smiled at her shrewdly, his gold tooth on display, reminding her of their conversation.

"Okay, well, I'll see you then."

Grinning, she grabbed the silver door handle to let herself out. When she did, he reached across the seat, grabbing her arm.

"There's something special about you, Sarah. You're gonna be one of my best girls. If there is anything you ever need, just let me know. Remember, I told you I'll take care of you. I meant that. You understand me?" He increased the grip on her arm.

"I understand, Wallace," she said, not quite knowing how to react.

"Call me WB."

"What's the 'B' for?"

"Bynum. My last name is Bynum."

"Okay, WB. I'll see you next week," she responded coyly, then got out of the car and closed the door.

Sarah turned her key in the door as quietly as she could, as Wallace's car pulled off. Once inside, she saw Brady, fully dressed, with his boots on, asleep on the couch in the front room. It appeared as though he had passed out. Trying not to wake him, she tiptoed up the stairs. The creaking noise each step made rang out like a symphony, but she managed to make it to her bedroom without him knowing. When she closed the door, she was happy and relieved, like she had made a successful slide into home base at the end of a big game. Exhausted, she quickly stripped out of her clothes and got into bed. Her head sank into the pillow. She exhaled deep and fell asleep, thinking about the kiss she and Wallace had in the storage room.

✂

It was Monday morning and the last day of school for the year. Sarah hadn't heard from Rita since Saturday when they dropped her off. When she didn't knock on the front door at 7:30 a.m. sharp, for their normal walk to school, Sarah knew it could only be because she was still upset. When Sister Anne rang the bell for the class to recess and go outside for lunch, Sarah was surprised again when Rita didn't come join her at their regular table under the big cedar tree. They always ate their sandwiches together, but not today. She watched Rita from across the yard as she ate with some of the other girls.

After school, Sarah ran to catch up with her on the way home.

"Are you still mad at me?" She was breathless when she caught up with her.

Rita never turned her head to look at Sarah. Instead, she kept walking with her focus on the country road ahead.

"Are you going back to that place?"

"Yes, on Friday."

"I can't believe you're going back there! I hope you know what you're doing, Sarah!"

"It won't be for long. I'm going to make a lot of money really quick so I can get out of this stupid town." Sarah struggled to keep up with her fast pace while trying to make her understand.

"If you come with me, we can both be out of here by harvest! You on your way to live with your papa and me headed to New York. What do you say?"

Rita was walking so fast.

"If working at that place is how you plan to get out of *here*, then leave me out of it! I would rather stay here the rest of my life than do what those bimbo girls in that place are doing with those men! You can't see that?" Rita huffed, winded from walking and angry from frustration with Sarah.

"Rita, everybody has to make their own choices, and this is mine. I understand if you don't want to do it, but as a favor to me, pleasssse don't tell anybody I'm working there. It'll be a secret between you and me, okay?" Sarah pleaded and pulled at Rita's arm, hoping she would stop walking.

Rita yanked her arm from her grasp but stopped and looked at her. She squinted her eyes at Sarah hard and long, her face conflicted with both love and scorn. Without a word, she turned and ran fast, just to get away.

⤞⤝

When Thursday came, Sarah was getting anxious about the weekend and worrying about going back to Youngstown for her first night of work. This time, she would be making the trip alone, and that made her even more nervous. She planned to tell Brady she would be at Rita's house again but this time for the whole weekend. She struggled all week with what to wear and what to pack in her small suitcase. She searched through her closet, but all she could find were schoolgirl skirts and sweaters and nothing that looked grown-up enough for a sporting girl.

Her mother's belongings were still in her room, exactly the way she left them. After almost five years, she and Brady had never gotten rid of her things. Sometimes when she was feeling sad and missing Lucy, Sarah would go into her mother's room, open her closet, and stand there a long time, leaning into the jasmine scent she wore that still lingered on her clothes. That day, Sarah dug deep inside the closet and found an A-lined emerald-green dress hanging way in the back. It was gorgeous. She had never seen it before. And it looked new and fancier than anything she ever saw her mother wear. The fabric had a glittery sheen, which made it even more special. When she tried it on, it fit her body perfectly and in all the right places. She wondered where her mother had worn it or if she ever did. Maybe she had gotten it for a party she never got to go to, with the beautiful, rich friends she never got to meet, in a life she never got to live.

"I won't let that happen to me, Mama," Sarah whispered.

❧

She was in line at the bus stop at 6:00 p.m.—along with the people getting off work from the mill who were heading back home to Youngstown. She decided to wear the same blue skirt she wore the week before but this time with a black sweater that was buttoned up to her neck. It was her plan to open a few of the buttons on the sweater before she got to the house to look more womanly and experienced. But knowing she was making the trip alone and the neighborhood she would have to walk through, she decided it was probably best to draw as little attention to herself as possible until she got where she was going.

The same driver was behind the wheel as before. When she boarded, he recognized her.

"Hello, young lady. Where's your friend?"

"She couldn't come this time."

Sarah was hoping he wouldn't ask her any more questions.

Rather than sit in front like they did last time, she moved to the center of the bus and sat down quietly beside a lady who had her eyes closed with her head against the window. She appeared asleep by the exhausted, drawn looked on her face. The serene bus ride gave Sarah plenty of time to manufacture all sorts of ideas in her head about what would be waiting for her in Youngstown.

Chapter 7

A huge orange sun was beginning its crescent descent in the western sky as Sarah headed down the hill toward Livingston Street. This time, she knew where she was going, so she walked faster and with more confidence than she had just a week earlier with Rita.

I can do this! She smiled when thinking to herself.

In a few months, I'll be out of here! And nobody has to know where I got the money to do it.

With each step, she felt more grown-up and in charge of her life. She swelled from the sense of making her own way in the world. When she got to the intersection, she didn't waste any time crossing the street and heading south down Livingston. At the corner with the neighborhood bar, two colored men were standing outside, talking to each other and smoking. They were so focused on their conversation that they didn't notice her coming toward them until she was right at the corner and ready to cross. When they did see her, they stared surprised, first at each other and then back at her. The lighter one of the two let out a cat whistle meant for her.

"Hey, white girl, what you doing down here?" the other one yelled out.

Sarah acted like she didn't hear them. She didn't look their way or say anything. Seeing that no cars were coming, she quickly crossed the street, walked past them, and continued her deliberate pace. After two more blocks, she came to the dilapidated section of houses where the incident with the woman with the black eye happened last Friday. Luckily, this time, there was no one on the street. The only sign of life was a big black dog tied to a stake in his owner's yard. It barked and growled at her through the chain-link fence that surrounded the house. Crossing over another block, in the distance, she could see the green and white awning of the front porch at *520*. Her heart began racing. In preparation, she put her suitcase down on the ground, unbuttoned the top two buttons on her sweater, and ran her fingers through her loosely flowing hair. When she neared the gate, the pounding in her chest grew harder.

This is it. There's no turning back. It repeated over and over in her head. Her hands were shaking when she lifted the catch on the gate. She was frightened beyond belief. But her fear didn't stop her from opening it and walking in.

The two men who were standing at the door last Friday were on the porch in their black suits. When she walked up the green-painted concrete steps, the Caucasian one stepped forward to meet her.

"Good evening. I see you're back." His welcoming, John Wayne sort of smile, made his gigantic size less intimidating.

"Ugh, hi, WB told me to meet him here at seven."

"What's your name?" he asked.

"I'm Sarah, Sarah Ruford."

"Oh, you're Sarah." He seemed somehow surprised when making the connection. "WB told us you were coming. Welcome. You're starting tonight, right?"

"Yes."

"My name is Harry, and this is Ben," he said, pointing. "Come on in. Let me get that bag for you. I'll let Wallace know you're here."

He took the suitcase from her hand. She walked onto the porch, following his outstretched arm that directed her to the front door. Her nerves were calmed by his kindness.

"Ben, I'll get her settled and be right back."

"No problem. Take your time. It's still early." Ben was husky and muscular like his buddy but appeared to be a man of few words.

When she stepped in the foyer with Harry, scenes from the previous Friday flashed back at her: couples dancing, the conversation in Shirley's room, Miss Betty at the desk, the storage room with Wallace. It was all real again.

"Sarah, why don't you wait in here? I'll go get the boss."

"Okay."

Harry pointed her to one of the tables in the parlor. He put the suitcase down next to it and went down the back hallway toward the storage room. Sarah sat nervous and quiet and waited in the huge house, which was now strangely still. The only sign of the bustling place it had been a week before was the stale smell of cigarette smoke that still dominated the air. The mute of the house was made eerie by the diminishing light of day. The last moments of the sun came bright through a second-floor window, creating a spotlight on the red steps of the staircase and put the rest of the downstairs, including her, in the shadows.

After a few minutes, she heard the sound of Wallace's baritone voice. He was talking to someone down the hall. At the same time, the front door opened, and Shirley walked in, laughing with another girl. She looked older than Shirley, and though her skin was chocolate, she had straight blond hair that fell to her shoulders. Sarah couldn't help but stare because she had never seen anyone like her before. They both wore narrow skirts that clung tightly to their stomachs and backsides, like the ones Sarah loved from the magazines. The black cardigan Shirley was wearing beautifully matched her yellow skirt. Four buttons were opened at the top of her sweater, exposing her bountiful cleavage. Their faces were heavy with makeup—their lips bright red, and their cheeks blushed and rosy. Each carried an overnight bag. As they came into the foyer, Shirley saw Sarah sitting in the parlor.

"Look who's here! You came back," she said, walking toward her with a mildly excited tone in her voice. "What's your name again?"

"Sarah."

"Right, I remember now. This is Iris. She works here too."

"Hey, how you doing?" the cutting edge in Iris's voice was anything but friendly. She looked at Sarah dismissively and proceeded to put her belongings down on one of the tables.

"You here for the meeting?" Shirley asked when she sat down at the table across from Sarah. She took a cigarette from the pack in her purse and put it to her lips.

"Meeting? WB just asked me to be here at seven."

"It's probably for the meeting. We all meet every Friday night at seven so WB and Miss Betty can tell us what we need to know about the weekend. It's a house rule to be here, so you'll get to meet everybody."

While Shirley was talking, Wallace walked in from the hallway, handsomely dressed in a dark blue suit, white shirt, and navy tie. Harry and Sam followed him. When he spotted Sarah, a big grin came across his face. Sarah stood to her feet, nervous but excited to see him.

"There's my girl! Everybody, this is Sarah." He put his arm around her shoulders. "She's starting tonight. She's gonna make us a whole lotta money!" he said excitedly.

Sarah was happy he was glad to see her but uneasy with the way he was making her the center of attention.

"Where's she settin' up shop, WB?" Iris asked, aggravation in her voice as she leaned over the table toward him. "'Cause I ain't giving up my room for nobody." She rolled her eyes, sat back in her chair, and crossed her arms.

"You'll do whatever the hell I tell you, Iris!" Wallace snapped at her sharp. Sarah's eyes got wide and unnerved by how quickly he became aggressive. "Don't start nothing with that attitude. You don't even know her yet."

"All I know is we got another white girl here to take business away from the rest of us." Irritated, Iris rolled her eyes again and turned her head, slinging her blond hair back to one side.

The front door opened again, and two more attractive girls—one white and one Negro—walked in. Both were in full makeup and dressed in fashionable clothes, like Shirley and Iris. When he saw them come in, Wallace raised his arms and opened them wide, as if to welcome everyone. "Great! The family is all here."

"What's going on, WB?" the one with porcelain skin said as she walked over to where they were gathered.

"Loretta and Barbara, this is Sarah, the new girl. She's starting tonight."

When hearing her name, Sarah remembered Loretta was the one who lived in Warren and had a car. The two women curiously

NOBODY'S CHILD

looked her up and down without saying a word. Not wanting to appear intimidated, Sarah did her best to stand her ground but cowered from a lack of confidence and couldn't look either of them in the face for very long the way they did her.

Loretta was glamourous like a movie star, with defined features, like a blond Judy Garland. Her lips were red and full, and something about her was sensible and mature. A beauty mole on her right cheek added subtle sophistication to an already pretty face.

"How old is she, WB?" Barbara asked. She sat down, crossed her caramel arms over her chest, and smirked her mouth to one side, still staring at Sarah. Barbara was petite with short black hair that was cut in a bob. Though her hair was short, it was fine and silky in texture. She had striking brown eyes, which gave her face a radiant softness, yet everything about her exuded sureness and strength. She wasn't as rude as Iris, but she didn't make Sarah feel welcome either.

"She's twenty-two. Any more questions?" said Wallace, annoyed.

When Sarah heard him tell the others her age, she remembered the lie she and Rita told him last week. She cringed to think what would happen if he knew she was only seventeen.

If I can make it to my birthday without him finding out, maybe it won't matter.

About that time, Miss Betty walked in from the back hallway with the young boy from last week following close behind. When she saw Sarah, she turned and looked at Wallace.

"Looks like we got us another one, huh, Wallace?"

"We sure do, Betty." The sound of his voice indicated how pleased he was. "Okay, everybody, take a seat so we can get started. Harry, tell Ben to come on inside."

Once they were all there, Wallace formally introduced Sarah as the new girl. He told them that she was from Warren and how she and her friend had been there the week before. He made a joke about the friend not coming back, but Sarah had gotten bitten by the place. None of them laughed. He said that she had a lot to learn, and he expected everybody to make her feel at home and help show her the ropes.

67

"Is that understood?" he said sternly, looking around the room at everybody as they sat in silence.

"You can count on me, Mr. Wallace, sir," said the young boy whose name was Bobby.

"I know I can count on you, Bobby. It's these ladies I'm worried about."

Loretta reached over and touched Sarah on the arm. "You'll be okay, don't worry. We're all family here, and we look out for each other." Sarah appreciated the kindness because she had been shown very little of it since she arrived.

"You still ain't told us which room she gon' be in," Iris said, still concerned that she might have to give hers up.

"Miss Betty, what room we got available?" Wallace asked.

"She can take number three. It ain't been used for nothing but card playin' since Anna left," said Betty.

Sarah remembered Shirley saying Anna was the girl who got pregnant and the baby was taken away after she delivered.

"Be careful in that room, Sarah. A girl can get pregnant in there," Barbara said with a deceptive laugh as she looked at Loretta. Shirley and Iris laughed too.

"Miss Betty, anything you want to tell these ladies about tonight?" Wallace took a seat and gave her the floor.

She rose from her chair slowly like an elder and loudly cleared her throat to reestablish order.

"Speaking of getting pregnant...all y'all need to make sure you have a good supply of them rubbers in your room. I can't tell you that enough. If you need some, let Bobby here know and he can run 'em up to you. We've had a pretty good record since Anna left, so let's keep it going. Another thing... I know I've done said this before, but make sure you wash up good after your customer leaves. This place has a reputation for clean girls, so keep it that way! We don't need word getting out 'bout no disease spreading round here. I think that's everything I got to say, Wallace."

"Okay, thanks, Miss Betty." Wallace got up to make his own announcements. He talked about a convention that weekend at the hotel on West Street that would draw a lot of people looking for a good time. Harry would be spreading the word that *520* was the best party in Youngstown.

"You girls need to be ready for a busy weekend. Keep it clean, and let's make some money."

"Sometimes these convention people get a little crazy, WB. Harry and Ben got us covered, right?" Barbara asked, as she smacked on the gum she was chewing.

"Damn, right! If any of these johns get out of line, push the button and either Harry, Ben, or me will be up in a flash to kick their ass and throw them the hell outa here."

Hearing that, Sarah nervously raised her hand as if she were at school.

"Sarah, you got a question?" Wallace asked.

"What's the button?"

"Every room has a red buzzer on the wall right next to the bed. If you need help, push it, and it will buzz down here at the desk." He pointed across the foyer toward Miss Betty's desk.

"Oh, okay." She was frightened at the thought of being alone in a room with a man she didn't know and needing to push that button for help.

"Sounds good to me, WB." There was an unexplainable air of refinement in everything about Loretta.

"I'm good too as long as they come with a lotta cash," Shirley said. She smirked and smiled at Iris, who winked back at her in agreement. Sarah could see they were friends.

"Okay, anybody got any questions?" Wallace prepared to end the meeting. "All right then, let's have a good night."

Sarah remained seated as everyone else got up, put their chairs back in place, and began dispersing. Shirley put out her second cigarette in the ashtray, gathered her things, and along with Iris and Barbara, headed toward the stairs. Loretta was getting ready to do the same when Wallace came over to where she and Sarah were sitting.

"Hold on, Loretta, I need to talk to you a minute."

"Yeah, boss?"

"Sarah here lives in Warren and needs a ride. Can you help me out with that?"

"Yeah, sure. Where do you live in Warren, Sarah?"

"My house is just off Main Street, on Crane."

"Crane, yeah, I know where that is. Barbara rides with me too and gives me thirty-five cents a week for gas. That work for you?"

Sarah thought about all the money she would be making.

"Yes, that sounds fine."

"I can pick you up on Friday and take you back on Sunday."

"That will work just fine. Thank you!"

"Okay then. I'm gonna head upstairs. Let me know if you need anything, Sarah. I'm in number one."

"Thanks, Loretta." Sarah was glad at seeming to have made at least one friend in this house of strangers.

After Loretta went upstairs, Sarah and Wallace were alone in the parlor. Her heart beat fast, wondering what was going to happen next.

"What happens now?" she asked.

"You and I need to spend a little time together. Why don't we go upstairs to the office?" he said, grabbing her suitcase.

"Okay."

She didn't know what would happen in the office, but she was scared.

This must be the training he talked about. She could barely keep her legs from shaking.

As they left the parlor and started up the stairs, Miss Betty came from the back hallway carrying a square box she held with both hands.

"You gon' be a while, Wallace?"

"Yeah, I'll let you know when I'm free."

"Okay, I'll have Bobby work on gettin' number three ready. He'll have it cleaned up and ready by the time you're done."

"Sounds good."

Sarah went with him up to the top of the stairs and followed him to the office. He took his key ring from his pocket. When he had unlocked the door, he pushed it open with his hand, stood to the side, and let her walk in ahead of him. Once inside, he closed the door and turned on the desk light. Sarah remembered the masculine design of the room with its dark wood and leather furniture. The masculine smell of the cologne he wore was faint in the air. She looked at his desk and thought about the small door in the wall behind it that had revealed the man and woman in the next room. Now that she had met all the girls, she realized the woman she and Rita watched through the wall was Iris. The room next to the office was hers.

"Make yourself comfortable," Wallace said, pointing to the couch that was adjacent to the desk. "Let me fix you a drink."

He headed to a small shelf in the corner that was filled with bottles of different sizes and colors. At the same time, he took off the jacket to his suit and tossed it across a brown high-back chair that was nearby. With one hand, he unbuttoned the top of his shirt, loosened his tie, pulled it from around his neck, and neatly laid it on top of the jacket. The crisp white shirt he had on underneath clung to his body and complemented the definition of his arms and chest.

Sarah kept her eyes on him and nervously sat down on the brown leather couch. When she saw the developed outline of his body through his shirt, she got excited and felt an unexpected quiver around her waist.

"Let me see if I remember. You and your friend both like whiskey. Did I get that right?" He stared at the bottles with his back toward her as he spoke.

"That sounds fine." She thought about the dizzy feeling she and Rita had last week when they drank it.

Wallace poured two glasses of a brown liquid. Afterward, he put the top back on the bottle, grabbed the glasses, and went and sat down on the couch next to her.

"Here's to making lots of money!" he joked, handing her a glass as he made the toast. Clanking his glass to hers, he raised it to his mouth, let his head drop back, and emptied it. Sarah tried to do the same, but the strong drink got caught in her throat, and she began coughing and choking.

"Slow down now. You don't have to rush. A good woman knows how to take her time with a man." Patting her back, he tried to help her catch her breath. It took a few seconds, but she was finally able to calm down and stop coughing.

"Okay, now take a slow sip," he told her. When she did, it helped settle her throat.

"That's better," she admitted.

"Take another sip."

She followed his instructions like a student.

"So you saw last week what the girls do here to make money. After you told me you were a virgin, I had to think about what to do with you. I can't expect a virgin to satisfy customers the same way Iris, Shirley, and the other girls do. You need training, and lots of it. I want to teach you, so when the time comes and you're ready to be with a customer, you'll know what to do."

"Okay, WB, whatever you say." She was warmed by his being so kind and thoughtful.

Wallace put his glass on the table beside the couch, then took the one out of her hand and placed it beside his. Light-headed from the drink, the anxiousness she felt earlier was completely gone. It was about to be her first time, but because it was him, she felt ready.

Turning back toward her, he grabbed and pulled her close and kissed her lips long and slow. Gradually, the intensity increased, and he let his tongue begin exploring hers.

"Kissing is just for you and me. Don't put your tongue in the mouth of none of these johns, you hear me?" he spoke low but direct.

"Yes" was the one-word response she gave as she fell deeper under the seduction of the moment. Everything faded to a blur, and her mind and body became an ocean of senses; the feel of his chest and his arms, that distinctive scent he wore, the hazel in his eyes as he kept his gaze on her—it was more than perfect.

When he unbuttoned her sweater, the quiver she felt earlier intensified and commenced to come in waves. She became aware of her breath and how loud and rapid it had become, but she couldn't control it. Through a fog, she vaguely remembered Wallace removing his shirt and hearing the jingle of his belt buckle. Before she knew what was happening, she was lifting her hips, and he was removing the last of her clothing. He stopped momentarily and reached for a rubber from the drawer in the side table.

"Never without one of these," he told her quietly, as he skillfully opened the packaging with his teeth. The pain was momentary, but the feel of him and the closeness of his body made her feel wonderfully consumed. She didn't want it to end.

⊱⊰

The whole thing was relatively quick, and when it was over, Wallace sprang to his feet and pulled up his trousers without saying a word. Sarah, still overcome, didn't know whether to feel good or horrified by the incident. Seconds passed with him attending only to himself, not looking at her, or saying anything. The sudden change in him created angst that quickly made her feel dirty. She sat up and grabbed her sweater from the floor and used it to cover herself. Tears, she didn't want him to see, came easily.

"*Sarah! What on God's earth have you done!*" It was Head Mother's voice shouting and scolding her from someplace in the distance.

It made her panic! *What have I done! He must not have felt what I did or feel the way I do now. He acts like that was nothing!*

"*Sarah! Silly girl! What did you think was going to happen?*" It was Sister Anne. "*Have you forgotten everything we taught you at St. Bernadette?*"

"That was a good first time," Wallace eventually said when he broke the silence. "You're gonna need a lot more training, though. You're not ready for customers yet."

Putting on his shirt, he walked over to the chair to get his jacket and tie. When she realized this had been a lesson and that it was now over, she got up from the couch, wiped her teary face with the back of her hand, trying not to let him see. She buttoned her sweater and smoothed down her skirt. Still shaking, she ran her fingers through her hair to tidy it. When she was put back together, she happened to look down at the leather on the couch and saw a smeared red stain. When she saw it, she put her hand to her mouth, startled.

Wallace noticed her shock. "Don't worry none about that. Miss Betty will send Bobby to take care of it." The thought of Bobby having to clean up the mess they had made added to her embarrassment.

When he was fully dressed, he did a final check of himself in a wall mirror and then quickly patted down his pants and breast pocket, making sure he wasn't forgetting anything. By then, Sarah had steadied herself and moved to sit in one of the chairs in front of the desk. She waited for what was next. Wallace came over and put his hand on her shoulder.

"Like I said, that was good. For a minute there, I got to admit I almost forgot I was with one of my girls." He said it as if to make a joke, but the subtle catch in his voice and the way his brow wrinkled reflected something else.

He moved his hand from her shoulder to under her arm where he applied gentle pressure, bringing her to her feet.

"I can see right now you're going be my special girl." Holding her head in his hands, he put his face so close to hers their foreheads touched.

"You need more time, though, to get settled in and more practice. In the meantime, I'll find some other things you can do around here. We're shorthanded downstairs, so I'll have you work down there with Sam tonight."

"Okay, but I'll still get paid, right?" She remembered why she had come in the first place.

"Of course, you'll get paid. You'll have to earn every penny too!" he responded playfully, tapping the tip of her nose with his finger.

Bending down, he grabbed her suitcase and opened the door. "All right then, let's get out of here and go make some money."

Chapter 8

When Wallace opened the door, the big band sound of Bennie Goodman came blasting in from downstairs. It was eight-thirty, and over the banister, they could see that a dozen or so people had arrived. Some were seated at the tables, and a few were standing around the bar, where Sam was busy making drinks. A hazy cloud of cigarette smoke was rising in the parlor and slowly making its way out into the open space of the foyer. Miss Betty was at her desk and looked up and saw them when they came out of the office. Bobby sat quietly, occupying himself on a high wooden stool behind her. He was swinging his feet like a child while flipping through what appeared to be a comic book. She leaned back in her chair and said something to him. Immediately, he jumped off the stool and ran up the stairs toward them.

"The room is ready, Mr. Wallace," he said, out of breath when he reached them.

"Okay, thank you, Bobby."

They followed as he led the two of them pass the big clock and down the left hall. He was only a boy, but a shuffle in his walk resembled one of a man racked by age. Looking down at his feet, Sarah could see that one of his shoes had a heel that was much higher than the other one. When they got to the door with number 3 on it, he opened it with his key and stood to the side to let them walk in.

"Miss Sarah, you need anything, just let me know, and I'll come runnin'."

"Thank you, Bobby." He was as nice as could be. He handed her the key and quickly disappeared.

The room was decorated in varying degrees of purple, from dark to light. The color purple just so happened to be her absolute favorite! They learned in school that it was a sign of royalty. After that discovery, the color became special to her and, as a result, always made her feel safe. She smiled warmly when entering the room and seeing it displayed so prominently. Purple also reminded her of all things good. During one of their Bible classes, Sister Anne spoke to them about Jesus's last days and how the people covered him with a robe of purple. "King of the Jews!" they yelled.

When Sister retold how willingly He died that day, Sarah sat at her wooden desk and listened mesmerized, tears streaming down her face. The color also brought to mind her grandma, Eleanor, and the purple teddy bear she'd given her for Christmas that one year. It was an unlikely color for a bear, but over the years, its cuddly cuteness became a source of comfort. She named him King because, despite his outer furriness, his character was strong like a lion. Long after she became a teenager, King stayed a close confidant and a nonjudgmental listener to all her hopes and dreams.

The shiny bedspread was deep and dark, almost grape. Three pillows of lavender were at the head. She immediately saw the big red call-for-help button Wallace talked about at the meeting. It was on the wall within comfortable reach of the bed and stood out in sharp contrast to the other colors in the room. There was also a comfy-looking high-back chair in the corner covered in a fabric of lilac and white wildflowers. A round table that must have been the one used for playing cards was pushed to another corner, and a lavender cotton cloth covered it. A vase of fresh spring daisies was placed tastefully in the center. It was way nicer than her room at home, and she was overjoyed that it would be hers.

"I need to get going, Sarah," Wallace said. "You'll waitress and help Sam at the bar tonight. Be sweet and mingle with the customers. Make 'em wanna go upstairs. Anybody ask for you, let them know you're a hostess and they need to see Miss Betty at the desk. I'll have her send you up a uniform. You look like a size six to me. What size shoe do you wear?"

"Size seven," she said in one of her silly schoolgirl giggles.

"Okay then, I'll check in on you a little later."

When he closed the door, she was so relieved to finally be alone. It felt as though she had been holding her breath for hours and could finally exhale. Falling backward onto the bed, she stared up at the white ceiling, dazed. It had only been a few hours, but in that short time, everything had changed. She instinctively knew she wasn't the same person she was when she arrived earlier that evening. The feeling was indescribable. It was as if a blinder she had been wearing was ripped from her eyes, and everything looked and felt different. The girl who arrived for the seven o'clock meeting had strangely disappeared, and she was disoriented at the realization that she was gone.

You should not *stay here, young lady! Leave while you still can!*

As clear and jarring as Head Mother's voice was, the spell Wallace had placed her under was more compelling.

He called me his special girl. She smiled broadly at the thought of being *special* to such a powerful, handsome man.

I think I may be falling in love with him.

What if he's falling in love with me too? Young and naive, she loved the idea that it might be true.

She got up and went to the mirror on the bureau and stared long at an image that was unlike the one she remembered.

I hope I'm doing the right thing, she wondered.

"God, you know how much I want to leave Warren." Looking in the mirror, she broke the silence and spoke the words aloud.

"Sister Anne and Head Mother are going to be proud of me someday. Just wait and see!" *All this will be behind me by August. And when I'm famous, it will be like none of this ever happened.* She renewed her vow to herself, fought back against any signs of doubt, and shifted her focus to other concerns.

Uncle Brady can never find out!

She was terrified, imagining the look on his face.

There's no telling what he would do.

"This is my life now, and I can't worry about what other people think. It's my only chance to get out of this place!" she spoke with conviction.

With a burst of energy, she put her suitcase on the bed and opened it. While unpacking her things and putting them in the bureau drawer, she flashed back to being with Wallace, reliving all the sensations she had when they were together. As she waited for a sound at the door and someone to tell her what was to happen next, she sat on the edge of the bed, put her head back, closed her eyes, and dreamed of him.

Out of nowhere, there was a purposeful knock on the door. When she opened it, Bobby stood there smiling and holding a short black dress on a wire hanger. It had a white lace collar and appeared cleaned and pressed. In the other hand, he held a square cardboard box.

"Hi, Miss Sarah. Mama said to bring this up to you."

Suddenly it made sense that Bobby was Miss Betty's son. The fleeting resemblance between them was distinctly clear. Both naturally exhibited an irritated, down-in-the-mouth, frowned appearance. It was obviously a family trait. Difference was, happy-go-lucky Bobby, unlike his disgruntled mother, smiled much more than he didn't.

"Thank you, Bobby."

She took the dress from him with one hand and the box with the other.

"Mama said come downstairs when you ready."

"Okay, I will. Thank you."

A few minutes later, she was in the form-fitted hostess dress, the length of which barely covered her thighs. And with only two buttons in front, her developed youthful cleavage was fully pronounced. A delicate white lace around the open collar added a suggestion of innocence to an outfit that was anything but. In the box were sheer black thigh-high stockings and a modest pair of previously worn black patent heels. Even after putting on the stockings and pulling them up as high as she could, there was still a gap of several inches that exposed her bare white thighs. Luckily, they came up sufficiently high enough to cover the ugly scar on her thigh she got from the accident that day on the river three years earlier. She hated that scar and hoped Wallace hadn't seen it.

"Is this what a waitress wears?" she asked herself, young and confused.

When she first looked in the long mirror on the closest, she was sheepish. Never had she worn anything so skimpy. At St. Bernadette, a girl coming to school with a hem above the knee would have gotten five whacks across the knuckles with Head Mother's ruler. The thought of being on display in such an outfit in front of all those people—particularly men—made her face red with anxiety.

She tugged at the dress's hem to try to make it cover her legs and pulled tighter on the two front buttons, hoping to cover her chest more, but there was no use. The uniform was obviously made short to entice men. Petrified, she struggled to muster confidence. Taking several deep breaths, she imagined herself walking around downstairs with a tray of drinks in hand while the men in the room stared, watching her every move. Her heart was pounding.

The longer she looked at herself in the mirror, the more she was reminded that the scant, revealing little dress was actually a gift. It was prolonging her having to do what the job really required. The eventuality of being the one naked with the man in the room on the other side of the wall was more real than she ever thought it could be. She was in no hurry to transition to that role. The good news was she had gotten a job, was making money, and at least for now, hadn't done anything like what she and Rita saw the week before. Suddenly, the tight little dress was actually quite cute and really didn't show that much anyway.

So what if it shows a little leg? I look pretty. I hope WB will like it.

Without further hesitation, she washed her face in the basin, brushed her blond hair back into a ponytail, and put on her signature scarlet-red lipstick. After a few more deep breaths to steady herself, she opened the door to the sultry sounds of Billie Holiday. Her nerves were in a state of flurry when she turned and locked the door with her key. Carefully, she made her way downstairs.

More people had arrived, mostly men, and there was a buzz of activity as some folks drank and talked at tables while others moved about, mingling. There were more white men than there had been last week. Harry had clearly done a good job recruiting out-of-towners from the convention. And it was easy to see who wasn't one of the locals. Their pale-colored sear-sucker suits and conservative Army crew-style haircuts were distinctive. A noticeable contrast to the many Negro men in their dark suits and fedoras. In addition, they had congregated to one side of the room, separating themselves from the other customers. Clearing the bottom step, Sarah went over to Miss Betty, who was still seated at the desk.

"What do you think, Miss Betty?" she asked and spun around, full of energy. She was all smiles and hoping she could make friends with a woman who only seemed to wear a scowl.

Miss Betty took a pause from whatever she was writing in a leather book and looked up at her over her reading glasses.

"I guess you'll do," she said, expressionless, and went on with whatever she was doing.

It wasn't the response Sarah hoped for, and she was embarrassed for having asked.

"I think you look real pretty, Miss Sarah," Bobby blurted from his stool.

"Be quiet, Bobby! Nobody asked you nothin'!" she snapped at him. "Wallace wants you to see Sam at the bar and help him in there tonight. He'll show you what to do."

Sensing Miss Betty was in no mood for small talk, Sarah took her instructions and moved on through the crush of people toward the bar.

Sam was already having a busy evening and trying to keep up with the drink orders. Sarah joined him behind the bar so she could talk to him as he worked. When he saw her, he perked up and gave a smile.

"Yes, ma'am, I hear we working together tonight. Glad to have you! As you can see, I can use the help. You didn't bring your friend this time?"

Sam continued working—moving around, mixing this, pouring that. The limp he managed while moving from one end of the bar to the other was interesting to watch, but it didn't slow him down.

"No, it's just me tonight. What can I do to help?" Sarah raised her voice so he could hear her over the roar of the room. She was quick to change the subject, not wanting to explain more about why Rita wasn't with her.

After Sam finished serving a skinny tall man and his loud, tipsy, overweight female companion, he took a break to teach Sarah what to do. He gave her a small white pad of paper and said to write down the drink orders in a way she would know who got what.

"Write down words that describe the person," he told her. "Like write *bald* next to an order for whiskey. That way, when you come back with the drinks, you know the bald man at the table ordered the whiskey. Got it?"

"Yes, sounds easy enough," she told him.

He also showed her how to carry a tray full of drinks through the crowd without dropping it. She spent the next several hours moving through the crowd, going back and forth to the bar. She was friendly and nice to the customers just like Wallace told her, making small talk with many of them as she went about her work.

One man, who kept rubbing her hand when she put his drink down on the table, asked if she would go upstairs with him. Just like WB instructed, she sent him over to the desk and Miss Betty. Soon after, Sarah watched him go up the staircase and knock on Iris's door. She could see through the banister when Iris opened the door dressed in her pink robe. She grinned like she was happy to see him, took his hand, pulled him into the room, and closed the door.

A few times while Sarah was making her way through the sea of people, drink tray in hand, she felt a male hand up under her uniform. She learned quickly to pay little attention to it, realizing it was just something that came with the job. Most of the men, however, were gentlemen, but those from the convention were crumbs and behaved crude and vulgar. As they drank, their rudeness grew. One of them smoked a pipe and had a belly so round, two of the buttons on his shirt near his plump waist had popped open. He kept taunting her all evening and addressing her as "sportin'." He tried to be clever, using a short name for a sporting girl.

"Sportin'! What's a nice white girl like you doing in a place with all these niggers?" Sarah didn't answer and tried to put down their drinks and move on as fast as she could. But every time she brought drinks to their table, he pretended to drop his napkin on the floor and then asked her to pick it up.

"Sportin', can you get that for me?"

When she bent down to get it, he could get a much better view of her cleavage. The other two men at the table, with their cheap suits and crew hair, joined together in uproarious laughter every time it happened. They also leaned over the table and took a good look. By their fourth round, the first man had become so drunk that when she stood up from picking up the napkin, he grabbed her and started licking and kissing her about the neck and chest. It caught her by surprise and disrupted her balance to the point that she nearly dropped the tray she was carrying. Sarah wasn't aware, but Harry had been watching from the corner of the room. When she was grabbed, he was there in an instant. He moved fast, pulled him off her, twisted his arm behind his back, and forced the side of his shocked face down hard onto the table and held it there. The other two men stood up fast to their feet, backed up, and did nothing to help their friend. Harry's enormous size and strength were enough for them not to challenge him.

"This young lady is here to serve drinks only. If you want something else, you need to see the lady at the desk. Do you *understand?*"

He was calm and clear and waited for an answer while continuing to keep a firm hold on the back of the man's neck.

"Yeah, yeah, I got it!" he yelled.

When Harry let go of him, the man stood up, rubbing his neck. The scene drew everyone's attention, and he was embarrassed by being the center of it.

"Let's get out of here," he said to his friends, still red and breathless from the force of Harry's handling.

In anger, the three of them threw several bills of money on the table to cover their drinks and then shuffled their way out the front door.

"Everything is fine, folks. Go back to enjoying yourselves," Harry told the crowd.

"You all right, Sarah?" he asked, looking at her closely in the face and helping her steady her hold on the tray.

"Yes, I'm fine. Thanks for looking out for me."

"That's my job. We're here to make sure you ladies stay safe."

About that time, Wallace came in from the back hallway. Just as he rounded the bar, the desperate sound of a woman screaming rang throughout the house. It was coming from upstairs. Harry reacted immediately, running toward the stairs with Wallace following close behind. Miss Betty yelled to them, "Shirley, ringing for help!"

It meant she had pushed the red button in her room. They sprinted up the red stairs two at a time, rushing to Shirley's rescue. The commotion caused activity downstairs to come to a standstill as everyone looked toward the upper level.

When Harry and Wallace reached Shirley's room, they rushed through the door. The noise of a scuffle could be heard coming from the open door, but the action was out of view.

"You bastard!"

Wallace was clearly disgusted with whatever it was he saw.

The unmistakable smacking noise of fists hitting hard against skin poured from the room.

"Kill that piece of crap, WB!" screamed Shirley.

Whoever was the target of the brawl could be heard moaning as the punching continued. It reminded Sarah of the night Brady pounded on Vernon for forcing himself on her.

After a few minutes it ended, a strange quiet followed. Everyone downstairs was still fixated upward toward the room with the open door, waiting to see what had happened.

Chapter 9

After a few seconds, the silence was broken by the sound of Shirley's uncontrollable sobbing. It poured from the room and seemed to reverberate throughout the house. Her wailing was an expression of pain and sadness. The ache in her crying was almost tangible. Sarah felt sick to her stomach just hearing it. She wished there was something she could do to help. But she, along with the rest of the crowd, waited.

Finally, Wallace emerged through the doorway. There were noticeable red stains that looked like blood on his suit and white shirt. His face was taut and serious. He came over to the banister and leaned down.

"Miss Betty, we need you," he said with an anxious, exhausted voice, and motioned with his hand for her to come up to the room.

Betty quickly obliged and went up the stairs as fast as her wide hips and plump aging legs could carry her.

"Everything is fine, everybody. Go back to enjoying your evening," Wallace announced to the crowd.

By that time, the customers were becoming bored with the whole situation anyway, so they gradually went back to drinking and talking like they were before. Sam put Count Basie on the Victrola, and things quickly returned to normal. Sarah, however, was still curious to find out what happened to Shirley. She split her focus between serving drinks and keeping an eye on what was going on upstairs.

Barbara and Iris were without customers and had come out of their rooms, barefooted, both wearing their pink robes, to see what was going on. They made their way down to Shirley's door and waited outside. After several more minutes, Harry came out carrying a lifeless bleached-looking man, draped over his left shoulder. His clothing and hair identified him as one of the males from the convention. Sarah stretched her neck to try to get a better look at him, but it was hard to see from such a distance away. When Harry came around by the clock and headed toward the back stairs, she caught a glimpse of his bloody face. There was a gash in it near his right eye. Barbara and Iris stared at Harry and then the man when he passed by them with his heavy load, but no one said anything. When he was gone, the two of them rushed into Shirley's room.

It got later and later into the evening. Barbara and Iris eventually went back to their rooms and closed Shirley's door behind them when they left. Sometime later, Wallace came out, went down the hall, and also disappeared down the back steps. Miss Betty stayed in the room with Shirley.

Around 1:00 a.m., a distinguished older white gentleman with a salt-and-pepper beard and round spectacles arrived, carrying what appeared to be a medical bag. Relatively short in stature, he walked with a slight hunch in his back. Ben quickly escorted him up to Shirley's room.

By two o'clock, there were only four or five customers left in the bar, and Sam was beginning to clean up. Sarah helped by gathering all the empty drink glasses that were strewn about the room and wiping off the tables. Wallace emerged from the back, looking tired. He stood at the corner of the bar with his big arms folded across his chest and, for several minutes, stood watching the few remaining customers and appearing to be deep in thought. He had changed out of the bloody suit of clothes, removed his tie, and rolled the sleeves of a clean white shirt neatly up to the elbow. He went over to Sarah as she was clearing one of the tables.

"Everything go all right tonight, Sarah?" he asked, touching her on the arm.

The feel of his touch excited her, and she delighted in his being so close.

"Everything down here was fine, but I'm worried about Shirley. Is she okay?"

"She got beat up pretty bad. She has a black eye, and her lip is busted. That crumb she was with must have been on dope and just went off."

"Does that stuff happen all the time?" She clung to the hope that wasn't the case.

"Not all the time, but it can happen. Me and the boys are careful who we let come in here, but sometimes a crazy one slips through."

"Is she going to be all right?"

"She'll be fine, but she's gonna need to rest for a while, maybe take some time off. How much money did you make down here tonight?"

When he asked her, she dug into the side pocket of her uniform and pulled out her tip money, most of which was in change.

"I think I did okay!"

She had been busy serving drinks and hadn't paid much attention to the money she was putting in her pocket. There must have been at least three dollars, which she smiled, thrilled about.

Having had their last customers for the night, Loretta and Barbara came downstairs.

"Sam, can you please set up our bourbons? We need doubles tonight!" Barbara said loudly.

"You ladies have a tough evening?" He looked up at them from behind the bar as they approached. He stopped wiping the glasses he had just finished washing in a big round tub and placed two clean empty ones in front of them. They had on the clothes they had arrived in earlier that evening, but their makeup was all but gone, and their faces read of exhaustion. Sarah listened intently to their conversation as she put her tray of dirty glasses down on the counter.

"Tough doesn't begin to describe this evening," said Loretta. "One of my johns wanted me to act and talk like I was his mother. A real psycho!" She waited patiently for Sam to finish filling her glass with about two inches of bourbon, and then she took a huge gulp of it.

"I got into a spat with one of mine who wanted to use his necktie to tie me up," said Barbara. "Good thing I was able to calm him

86

down, or my face might be busted right now like Shirley's. That idiot did a number on her!"

"How was your evening, girls?" Wallace asked when he walked up.

"It was pretty good," said Loretta. Her tone changed about the evening when responding to Wallace. "But from what I heard, it sounds like Shirley's evening stunk."

"She's okay. Doc fixed her up, and she's resting. She got messed up with one of those cracker jokers from the convention."

Without elaboration, Wallace moved on and went about closing things down for the evening. He went behind the bar and counted the money in the strongbox while Sam washed glasses and sat them on the sideboard to dry. Sarah wiped the glasses he put out and talked to Loretta and Barbara as they got tipsy from their drinks. Eventually, all the customers called it a night and disappeared through the front door.

The later it got and the more Loretta and Barbara drank, the more they talked. Turns out, the two of them had known each other most of their lives. Barbara's mother, Big Barb, was a maid in Loretta's parents' house. She and her mama practically lived there. Barbara was just a year younger than Loretta, so the pretty little girls were playmates and confidants. Loretta had two older brothers, Chadwick and Steven, who never had time for their younger sister's silliness. So she and Barbara became like sisters. Her father was a bigwig at the mill in Pittsburgh. Constance, her mother, was a socialite and often entertained the couple's rich friends. Her father would sometimes have business people at the house, and they engaged in conversations that sounded important but flew over the heads of children. The constant activity kept Barbara's mother and their colored butler, Franklin, busy all the time. The girls were made to go out and play and stay out of the way.

Life wasn't so bad, though, at least not until Loretta's father started touching both of them when they were nine and ten. The father—whom, as a child, Loretta loved sitting on his lap and pulling on his curly beard—became a monster, making them both engage in unspeakable acts. He swore both of them to secrecy, saying what he did was a special gift for the two beautiful girls he loved.

On Loretta's fifteenth birthday, she had had enough and decided to tell her unsuspecting mother what her father had been doing to her for so many years. It was not news she took well. She didn't believe her. At fifteen, she grabbed her by the back of the head, drug her down the hall to the kitchen sink by her hair, and forcefully washed her mouth out with lye soap. When her father heard what had happened, he responded as if he were the victim and the target of his disturbed daughter's lies. At 10:00 p.m., on a cold Wednesday night in November, he told her to get the hell out of his house. She was given ten minutes to pack. When she came down the stairs with her suitcase, her father was standing alone, holding open the front door. She could hear her mother crying in the parlor, but she did nothing to stop it or help her. Grabbing her arm, he whispered in her ear, "You had to mess up everything."

Without a word, he put a wad of money in her hand and said, "Now get out!"

She walked through the open door, and he slammed it behind her. Barbara kept hidden but listened and saw everything that happened. When Loretta was sent to pack, Barbara did the same and grabbed whatever she could and quickly threw it into an old feed sack. When Loretta was forced out the front door, Barbara rushed out the back one. She left Big Barb a note that read,

> Gotta go with Loretta, Mama. This house is evil,
> and we can't stay here no more.
> I love you.
>
> Barbie

"I'm not letting you leave without me!'" she yelled at Loretta when she caught up to her a short distance from the house.

"Barbie! You'll come with me?" she asked through tears.

"Of course, you're my sister. Besides, I can't let you leave me here alone with that devil of a man."

The money Loretta's father gave her bought them two tickets on a late bus leaving for Cleveland. Loretta had a single female cousin there that was twenty-three and had her own place. It was small, but when they knocked on her door the next morning, she told them they could stay there a few days. They found jobs as waitresses at a bar where Wallace was the manager. He felt sorry for the two, being so young and on their own. He said he would look out for them. Customers loved the attractive pair, especially the men. Wallace kept a close eye on both and tried to make sure no harm came to the mature-looking yet still very young girls.

They developed fast while working there. Loretta liked the attention from the men. Despite Wallace's close watch, she began making side money engaging in sexual acts with them. The years of abuse with her father had prepared her well for knowing what men like and how to please them. Barbara had always been shy and reserved and was less willing at first, but when she saw how much money Loretta was making, she followed her lead like she had always done in the past and started doing the same thing. After they had worked there three years, the owner of the bar offered Wallace a job in Youngstown running a classy men's entertainment establishment he was opening there. The wealthy European owner had lots of investments, and Wallace was like a son to him. He trusted him with his business and his money. He jumped at the chance and took Loretta and Barbara with him to get the place started.

"So here we are, twelve years after we left my father's house in the middle of the night, still doing the same awful things we left there to escape."

Loretta's voice trembled with pain and regret. She looked down into her glass and the small amount of liquor left in it and turned it up to her head. Barbara saw that her sister-friend had gone to a dark place, so she reached over and tugged her arm.

"It's okay, sis, we did what we had to do to survive. We can't be blamed for that."

Chapter 10

On Saturday morning, the grinding noise of a sweeper, moving over the carpet outside her bedroom door, woke Sarah from a deep sleep. She sat up quickly and reached over and grabbed her mother's silver wristwatch from the table next to the bed.

"It's ten thirty!" She was shocked to see what time it was.

It was the first time she could remember ever sleeping that late. Usually, on Saturday mornings, Brady would have knocked on her door hours ago and called for her to get up and make breakfast before he left for whatever odd job he had lined up that day.

Realizing she wasn't at home and there was no need to rush, she let her head sink back into the linen softness of the lavender pillow. She bathed in the lazy comfy of the bed and her new room. A mid-morning sun was beaming in through the sheer white curtains of a half-opened window, and a gentle breeze was making them move with the wind. Exhaling, she melted into the coziness of it all. Staring up at the blankness of the white ceiling, she recounted everything that happened on her first night on the job in this strange place.

After Loretta and Barbara emptied their drinks and finished their storytelling, Sarah went up to bed with them around three thirty. Wallace and Sam were finishing the last of their chores when they said good night to them. When they got to the top of the stairs and the clock, Barb didn't hesitate in saying good night and headed straight for her room, quickly closing the door. But Loretta waited and talked to Sarah a little longer before calling it a night. They sat down next to each other on the top step and chatted beneath the ticking of the big clock. Loretta said Wallace lived in the backyard garage, which he had turned into an apartment.

"He's always around to make sure we're okay. If any of us ever need him, he's always close by. Miss Betty and Bobby live across the street in that gray house, the one with the screened front porch. She's always around too."

She sounded big sisterly and genuine in her attempt to make Sarah feel safe. If they had nothing else in common, the two of them were the only white females in the house, so for good or bad, that fact naturally connected them.

"Don't even think about getting close to WB." Loretta put her hand on Sarah's knee and looked at her stern and sober as if she knew she might already be falling under his spell.

"Me and Barbie have known him for years. As nice as he can be sometimes, he's all about business, making money and himself! He's broken lots of silly girls' hearts who wanted to believe he's something else. Don't you be one of them." Loretta turned and shook her index finger in Sarah's face to make clear her point.

Sarah went to her room, dejected after hearing that sweet, tender Wallace was the person Loretta said he was and not the kind, considerate, gentleman she had been with earlier that evening. She couldn't give up hoping that what happened between them was different, and he wasn't those terrible things Loretta said about him. It got even later, so they finally said their good nights. But when Sarah turned the key to the door of her new room, she was remembering how Wallace had called her his "special girl."

⁂

Around 11:30 a.m., there was a knock at the door that interrupted her sleepy daydreaming.

"Sarah, can I come in?"

It was Wallace. She sat up quickly in the bed, startled but excited.

"Just a minute!"

She leaped from the bed and, within seconds, had grabbed her robe from the back of the chair, splashed her face with water from the basin on the bureau, and ran a few fast strokes of a brush through her loose, full hair. When she opened the door, he stood there broad and manly and with a strange grin on his face. He was casual with an open collar, pressed, black shirt, and blue jeans. She was immediately impressed by how jazzy he looked, even in regular clothes.

"Sorry I kept you waiting," she said, breathless from all the rushing.

"You're even beautiful right out of bed." He walked in without waiting for an invitation.

"I thought we could get another lesson in before things get busy." He moved toward the bed and started unbuttoning his shirt. She could see that he was telling her what was about to happen and not asking for her permission. Either way, she was a willing participant.

Their short time together that morning was just as life-changing for Sarah as it had been the night before. However, this time, Wallace was much more intentional in coaching her on positions, movements, and touch. She was more relaxed and freer than the night before. He reminded her about the kissing rule, but yet again, he took full advantage of being the one exception to it and devoured every inch of her. When it was over, he fell back on the bed. He lay next to her, breathing deeply, with his forearm draped across his forehead and covering his eyes. Sarah lay there still with her eyes wide, staring at the ceiling. She tried hard not to become too anxious by his silence, like the way she had before.

When he finally stirred, he pulled her close so that her head was resting on his bare brown chest. Affectionately, he stroked her blond hair but didn't speak. She was loving the feel of their closeness and lay there, wondering whether he was feeling the same. After several minutes, he loosened his embrace and pulled her chin up so he could see her face.

"I don't know why, but for some reason, it's different with you. You got me feeling things I've never felt with a woman." He actually sounded vulnerable. "Truth is, ever since you and your friend came here last week, you've been on my mind."

She sat up on her elbows and looked at him, hardly believing what she was hearing.

Is it possible he really does have feelings for me? I just knew what Loretta said about him couldn't be true.

"I'm really not sure what to do about you," he said. "I gotta get you ready for these customers, but all that's on my mind is having you for myself. I got a business to run and no time for getting caught up like this and especially not with no girl that works for me."

By that time, he was clearly getting agitated and annoyed with himself. When he sat up on the edge of the bed with his back to her, he tugged and fought with his shirt, trying to get it on.

"You could probably use more training, but I can't keep being with you like this. You did good. You'll be fine with the customers. The other girls are a big help, so just ask them if you have a question, or you can ask me." He tucked his shirt back into his jeans.

Sarah's excitement fizzled when realizing he was trying to deny whatever it was he might have felt. She sat up in bed and watched him finish dressing. Pulling her knees to her chest, she grabbed the sheet and pulled it up under her neck.

"Tonight we'll see how you do. I'll have Miss Betty send you up a customer or two." Wallace secured the belt on his blue jeans and moved toward the door.

"Are you hungry?"

"Yes, I'm starving." She couldn't ignore that there was a rumble in her stomach.

He looked over his shoulder at her with one hand on the doorknob. "Miss Betty cooks a big breakfast in the kitchen on Saturday and Sunday mornings. Go down and help yourself. I ate a couple of hours ago."

"Okay, I will. Will I see you again before tonight?" she blurted out, anxiously hoping to keep him talking so he wouldn't leave.

He took a moment before responding, like he didn't know what to say. "You won't see me like this again," he said. "But I'm always around, so if you need something, let me know."

She sank when realizing this might be the end of a relationship that never really got started. Desperate to do something that could save it, she threw back the sheet and jumped out of bed.

"Don't leave without this."

Wallace was just about to open the door but turned to see what she meant. Quite out of character, she dashed bare body over to him. Without reservation, she wrapped her arms around his neck and, standing on her tiptoes, kissed him the way a woman kisses a man she's in love with. When it ended, he looked at her with his eyes wide, surprised by her aggressiveness.

"You're trouble, you know that?" he said, smiling. "You're gonna be just fine here. I'll see you later." He lightly kissed her forehead, opened the door, and left.

⬧

Sarah pulled her hair back into a ponytail and put on her plain black skirt and simple white short-sleeve blouse. She was glad that she had remembered to pack her oxford shoes; they were so comfortable. After wearing those black pumps all evening, her feet ached. When she was dressed, she looked more like the young inexperienced girl from Warren she was rather than the *sporting* woman she was about to become. She bounced down the back steps to the kitchen like a kid.

When she got to the bottom of the narrow curved staircase, she found herself face-to-face with Miss Betty, Iris, and Shirley. Miss Betty was at the sink in a yellow apron, washing dishes. Iris and Shirley sat near each other, eating their breakfast at a long dark wooden table similar to one you might use at a picnic. It was the dominant centerpiece in an otherwise modest kitchen. They all looked up when they saw her come in.

"Good morning!" Sarah announced chipper when her foot hit the last step.

"Well, look who's up," said Betty in her Southern drawl as she pulled a soapy plate from the water. "Thought you was 'bout to sleep all day."

"No, ma'am. I don't ever get to sleep late when I'm at home. So it was nice."

"You hungry?"

"Yes, ma'am, starving!"

94

"Well, get a plate and sit down there with Iris and Shirley, and I'll make you some eggs."

Sarah wasn't quite sure but thought she caught a glimpse of a smile on Betty's face when she told her to sit down.

"Thank you, Miss Betty."

Maybe politeness and respect is what she likes… I can do that.

If there was one thing she learned at Saint Bernadette's, it was to be respectful and have good manners. If any students spoke out of turn to one of the sisters, they could expect at least ten whacks across the knuckles with Head Mother's ruler. Her mother, Lucy, demanded respect as well. She remembered getting backhanded across the face when she was about ten years old for saying a new dress her mama bought her for the first day of school looked "stupid."

Sarah took a clean plate from the stack on the counter and sat down at the end of the table near where Shirley and Iris were seated. She was across from Shirley and Iris was at the head. Shirley was slowly trying to get a forkful of eggs passed her swollen lips and into her mouth. She was obviously in a lot of pain. Her right eye was bruised, black and swollen shut. Her left arm was wrapped up to the shoulder in an Ace bandage and held in place against her body by a white cloth sling that wrapped around her neck.

"Good morning," Sarah said when she sat down. "Shirley, I'm so sorry about what happened to you last night."

"Yeah, well, I guess I had it coming," she said in a low garbled voice. "Five years doing tricks and nothing like this ever happened."

"That don't make it right!" Iris said, mad. "No man should be able to beat up on a woman like she was some wild dog. I wished I coulda got a few licks in on that cracker!"

Miss Betty overheard the conversation and chimed in from over at the stove. "What you gon' do, Iris? You girls ought to know by now some mistreatin' comes with the territory."

"I left home tryin' to get away from mistreatin'. Swore I would never let no man beat up on me again," Iris grumbled as she poured a thick white gravy over the two open biscuits on her plate.

"You and me both," said Shirley. She cringed from the pain caused by opening her mouth too wide. She managed to get the eggs in her mouth and painstakingly chewed them against her sore jaw.

"I gotta feeling white girl here don't know nothing 'bout that." Iris leaned over and looked at Shirley but pointed her index finger at Sarah. "We here because this the only way we could figure out how to survive. Why you here, Snowflake?" Iris looked at Sarah with the same despise on her face she had when they met last night.

"I might not have been beat up by a man, but I've been poor my whole life. Me and my uncle can hardly pay our bills." That time, Sarah was the one who was mad. Iris was being rude to her and for no reason.

"My mama died because we didn't have enough money to get her proper medicals. No matter how hard she worked, she couldn't live her dreams. I'm not going to let that happen to me!" She was intimidated by Iris but gutsy and opinionated enough, in her own right, to stand her ground, especially knowing they were all going to be there in the house together.

"Is that your story, really?" Iris responded sarcastically and with a smirk.

"Girl, when I was eight years old, my mama started selling me to men so she could buy drugs to support her heroin habit. I started trickin' just so me and my little brother could have something to eat. One night, a man I was wit' beat me up bad and left me to die in an ally in Cleveland. If it wasn't for that sweet old woman that found me when she was putting out the trash, I wouldn't be here looking at you right now." Iris went from hard to soft when remembering the woman's kindness. "She was the sweetest woman I ever known. She took care of me for months like I was her own child. So that little story you telling about wanting some fairytale life, ain't nothing like what we been through." Iris poked her fork at Sarah in anger and to make her point.

After hearing Iris's story, Sarah didn't know what to say. She was still mad about the way she had talked to her but then felt sorry that her life had been so hard. It was clear to Sarah, at that point, that Iris was just mean, and she was never going to like her.

So what if my life hasn't been as bad as yours? I still have dreams!

Just in time to break the tension, Miss Betty came over with a plate steaming with scrambled eggs, bacon, and two of those opened biscuits covered in gravy. She removed the empty plate Sarah had gotten for herself and replaced it with the overfilled one in her hand.

"Eat up, girl," she said as she put the plate down in front of her. "You gonna need your strength. Look at me!" Miss Betty told her sharply. Sarah jumped a little when feeling the strength of the command in Miss Betty's voice. "Wallace done already been through here and told me you ready for upstairs tonight." She spoke with purpose and looked at Sarah close and in the eye to make sure she understood what the plan was for that evening. Iris and Shirley both looked up from their plates and grinned at each other. Sarah's face went white with fear.

WB had meant what he said. I guess I'm ready.

Shirley and Iris finished their breakfasts. Iris gathered both their empty plates and placed them over on the sideboard next to the dishpan.

"Come on, Shirley. Let's get you home," she told her friend.

"Okay, I just need to get Bobby to bring my bag down from the room." In pain, she was slowly getting up.

"Don't worry none 'bout your bag," said Miss Betty. "You two go wait in the parlor, and I'll call Bobby in from the yard and have him bring it down. You just take care of yourself, baby, and get well. Remember, Doc Southall said to take it easy for a while." She put her arms around Shirley and gave her the kind of hug a mother gives a daughter.

Quietly, eating her eggs, Sarah could see the genuine affection between them and longed to know what the secret was to Miss Betty's heart.

Chapter 11

Sarah ate everything on her plate and even had seconds of the bacon and biscuits. After breakfast, she retreated back to the solitude and comfort of her purple room, where she spent most of the afternoon alone, looking in the mirror and playing around with her hair. She experimented with a few different styles, trying to make herself look older, more sophisticated, and experienced—a sporting girl. In one version, she pulled it straight back and used bobby pins to pin it up in a bun on top of her head. She liked it and thought she looked like a young Katharine Hepburn—in a smart, sophisticated kind of way. Then she tried pulling it back on one side and held in place with a jeweled, sparkly butterfly clip she found in her mother's jewelry box. Both styles looked equally fetching, making it hard for her to decide which one would be right for the evening ahead.

Her hands were busy fussing with her hair, though she couldn't stop thinking about Wallace and the two times they were together. She lamented about if they would ever be together again. Her head was also spinning, worried whether or not she was ready to be just another one of the girls that night.

What will everybody in Warren think if they find out?

Sarah stared aimlessly and slowly brushed the hair on the right side of her head like she was paddling a boat that had gone adrift. The image of Iris and the man she and Rita watched her with through the opening in the wall was replaying over and over in her mind. It made her nervous thinking that in a few hours, that could be her.

When it was almost five o'clock, there was a knock at the door.

"Sarah, it's Loretta. Can I come in?"

She was stunned but happy to hear a friendly voice and scurried from the dresser over to the door.

"Hi, Loretta!" she said, excited.

Loretta was clean-faced in simple cropped pants and a printed blouse. It was a big change from the way she looked when they left each other the night before. Seeing her that way, Sarah felt like she was meeting her for the first time. She didn't seem at all like the glamourous film star she appeared to have been when they met. Instead, she looked surprisingly average, like someone Sarah could imagine herself being friends with, and she liked the change.

"I heard you're working upstairs tonight. I came by to see if you have any questions or need any help getting ready."

"Thanks," she said, opening the door wide and motioning with her hand for Loretta to come in.

"I was trying to decide how to wear my hair. What do you think?" Sarah turned her head from side to side.

"Let me help you."

Loretta had Sarah sit down on the stool in front of the mirror and began brushing her hair.

"Are you nervous about tonight? Since this is your first time and all. We all heard that you're a virgin."

"I'm not a virgin anymore!" Sarah responded as though she had to defend herself. "WB taught me," she said, strong and confident.

"Just so you know, your first time with a customer won't be anything like what you did with WB. The basics are the same, but a lot of these men have no respect for women and want you to do and say all sorts of things."

"I know," said Sarah. "I'm nervous, but I think I can handle it. Last week when I was here with my friend, WB let us watch Iris and a man through the wall in his office. It didn't look that hard."

"You seem like a nice girl, Sarah. Why are you doing this?" Loretta sounded concerned like the two of them had been friends for years.

"The rest of us are here because we didn't have any place else to go. We don't like what we do, but it's all we know. WB said you live with your uncle in Warren. I know the area where you live, and there are a lot worse places you could have come from. Are you sure you're supposed to be here?" Loretta stopped brushing Sarah's hair midstroke and waited for her answer.

"I know what I'm doing, Loretta." Sarah looked in the mirror and talked to Loretta's reflection standing over her. "Just because I haven't been beat up or taken advantage of doesn't mean I don't need money just like everybody else here. I've got big plans, and this is a quick way to make some money so I can get out of that dump of a town."

"Sarah, this is not some store clerk job you can just do for a while, move on, and forget about it. It leaves you feeling empty inside. I wish I could take back all the things I've done. I hate this life!" Loretta's voice broke, and her eyes watered. She lost focus and started brushing Sarah's hair faster and harder. Sarah turned around and grabbed her hand with the brush in it.

"You can still get out, Loretta! There are other jobs you could get."

"No, you don't understand. My daddy use to say, 'There's no easy money,' and he was right. It always comes with a price." Loretta shook her arm from Sarah's grasping hold and moved in close to her face—close enough that Sarah could see deep into the dark pupils of her sapphire blue eyes.

"Yes, you will make the money you want here, but you will *never*"—she paused—"be able to escape what you did to get it." She pointed a finger in Sarah's face.

"Thanks for the advice, Loretta. But don't worry about me." Sarah moved her head back and away. "I know what I'm doing. My dream is waiting for me out there I just know it! And I'll do whatever it takes to find it." She was surprised by her own confidence when she stood up from the stool and faced her.

"All right, but never say I didn't try to tell you."

Loretta stayed with Sarah all afternoon and helped her get ready. She went back to her room to get her makeup bag and expertly applied color to Sarah's eyes and lips the same way she and Barbara wore theirs. When she was finished, Sarah's hair was styled even prettier than the earlier versions she created herself. She still had a side sweep, but this one was much more fetching. The glittery butterfly hair clip was the icing on the cake to her seductive new older look. She could easily have been mistaken for a woman of thirty rather than a secretly young girl of seventeen.

"Okay, I better get going. I need to get ready myself."

Loretta hastily gathered up the lipsticks and eye makeup that were scattered across the top of the dresser and put all of it back in her bag.

"WB likes us downstairs on Saturday night by seven thirty."

Sarah barely recognized herself. She stared in the mirror, admiring herself in disbelief. She was oblivious to Loretta's moving about and talking as she collected her things, preparing to leave.

"That green dress will look nice with your hair and makeup," she told her and pointed to the dress hanging on the back of the door.

"It was my mama's," Sarah told her. "I'll wear it tonight if you think I should."

"You'll be a knockout in that dress! These johns won't know what hit them." She moved toward the door. "Wear it when you come down at seven thirty. WB likes us to mingle with the early arrivals. After that, you'll be up here in a pink robe like the rest of us and waiting for Miss Betty to send somebody up to your door." Sarah took the dress down from the hook. She quickly took off her skirt and blouse and began putting the dress on over her head.

"All right, I'll be down on time," Sarah said.

"Okay, see you downstairs." When Loretta opened the door, she was flabbergasted at suddenly being face-to-face with Wallace, who was just raising his hand to knock. "Good gracious! You just about scared me half to death, WB!"

"Loretta!" He was just as surprised to see her as she was to see him.

"I was just leaving to go get ready. I'll see you later, Sarah."

"All right, Loretta. Thanks for everything."

After she left and started down the hall, Wallace stood in the doorway, taking in his first look at gorgeous Sarah and her new look. He was ready for the evening and looked dashing in a bold purple suit—her favorite color—with a black shirt and tie. The familiar scent she found so intoxicating arrived when he did. Draped over his arm was a woman's pink satin robe.

"Well, well, well, what we got here!" He smiled, his gold tooth shining while he examined her from head to toe.

"Do you like it?" she asked, grabbing at the skirt of the dress on either side and twisting her hips.

"You look like a million-dollar dame! I'm losing my mind just looking at you."

"Thank you. I'm glad you like it." She sounded bashful.

"Like it? You look like a good steak!"

"Here, this is for you." He took the robe from his arm and handed it to her. It was silky and short, just like the ones the others wore.

"Come downstairs and entertain the guests. I'll let you know when it's time to get back to your room. That's when you need to put on the robe. After that, Betty will send up your first customer." His instructions were the same as what Loretta told her. "Remember everything I taught you. Use the rubbers and *no* kissing."

"Okay, WB. Whatever you say." When she reached to take the robe, he took her hand and used it to pull her close to his body.

"If any of these turkeys get even the least bit out of line, you push that button, and I'll be here in a flash, you hear me?"

Sarah just nodded fast and nervous. The time had come, and the job she came there for was about to start. She had to admit she was scared. The thought of having to push that button for help terrified her.

Before letting go of her hand, Wallace took advantage and kissed her, slow and passionately. It was a lover's kiss and not one an uncommitted teacher would give his student. When he let go, she was reeling, confused, unable to move.

He said we couldn't be together anymore?

"I won't let nothing happen to you. You're my special girl. You know that, right?" he said, holding both her shoulders. Not knowing what to make of the kiss or what he just said, she just nodded fast.

"Well then, I'll see you downstairs." He released his hold on her and quickly left the room. Sarah stood frozen, holding the pink robe in her hand.

I think I'm in love with him.

By 7:30 p.m., there were three or four men scattered around downstairs. When Sarah came down, she took her time scanning the room, taking note of everyone there. All but one of the early arrivals were neatly suited Negroes out for a good evening. The only white customer sat at one of the small tables near the window, drinking alone. Miss Betty was at her desk, shuffling through papers and looking busy. Ethel Waters was on the Victrola singing "Stormy Weather." Sam was behind the bar, unpacking a box filled with liquor bottles and storing them beneath the counter. Iris and Barbara sat together at one of the tables, keeping company with two of the colored men. When Sarah entered the room, she and Iris caught eyes. Iris was quick to divert her attention away from the laugh she was having with Barbara and the men and rolled her eyes at Sarah. Knowing she wouldn't be welcomed at their table, Sarah decided to go to the bar and check in with Sam.

"Evening, Miss Sarah," Sam said. He continued unpacking the bottles. "I hear we not working together tonight. Hear you done moved up to the big time!"

"I guess so, Sam. I hope I'm ready." She looked worriedly around the room at everyone there while she talked to him.

"You don't sound too happy. It's the job you wanted, right?"

Before she could answer, Wallace came in from the back hall. He and Sarah met eyes, but neither acknowledged the other.

"Boss, what you want me to do with that other box in the back?"

Sam and WB looked like they had business to take care of, so Sarah took the cue and went over to Miss Betty. When she neared the desk, the no-nonsense woman looked up over her glasses.

"Oooh, look at you all dolled up!" Miss Betty was expressionless, but still, it made Sarah feel good to think that she might have just given her a compliment.

"I think we gonna have another busy night. You think you ready?"

"As ready as I'll ever be, Miss Betty." Sarah put one elbow on the desk and stood there awkwardly looking around, pretending she wasn't scared out of her wits.

Bobby came in from the back, holding a stack of neatly folded white sheets in both arms and placed them on the table behind the desk.

"You look real pretty, Miss Sarah!" he said, looking at Sarah.

"Hush up, Bobby," Betty told him.

"Thank you, Bobby," Sarah said softly, not wanting to make trouble for him with his mama. However, she was grateful for the boost to her wavering confidence.

The front door opened with a gust of wind, and two young Negro men walked in. They came in laughing like they had just heard the punch line to a really funny joke. The one that was deepest in color appeared to be older. He was lean and lanky and particularly animated. He overused his body and his hands in the telling of whatever story it was that had them laughing so hard. Removing his fedora, he flung it at the hat rack near the door. When it landed on one of the hooks, he jeered like he had scored a goal. The younger one appeared much more reserved and seemed to be a little embarrassed by his loud companion. He looked around timidly, seeing if anybody was watching. Sarah saw them and recognized it as an opportunity to go over and try to entertain them the way Wallace had instructed.

When they picked a table and sat down, she went over and asked if she could join them. They both looked up, surprised, and the eldest was excited that she wanted to sit with them.

"Yes, ma'am, you can for sure sit your pretty self down here wit' us." He stood to his feet quickly and pulled out a chair for her. Wallace was helping Sam unpack the delivery, but Sarah could see over her shoulder that he was watching when she joined them.

They ordered drinks, and Sarah sipped what was fast becoming her usual: a whiskey shot. After nearly an hour, the party of three were feeling their drinks and having a grand time. Turns out, the two were brothers. Henry, the gregarious jokester, was out to show his shy baby brother, Willy, a good time for his twenty-first birthday. He bought a bottle of bourbon and commenced to pump him with drink after drink. Willy didn't say much, but he began slurring his words when he did.

"It's your birthday, li'l brother, so drink up!"

There was toast after toast.

They were easy to talk to, and Sarah was enjoying their company. When a Benny Goodman tune started playing, the conversation shifted to music. They all liked the same kind (Ellington, Bassie, Dorsey, etc.). Sarah remembered how the music blared on Saturday nights at their house and the way she sometimes danced with Brady's dizzy friends.

About 8:30 p.m., Henry leaned over, reached under the table, grabbed her knee, and slid his hand up under her dress. Sarah jumped in her seat, shocked at the sudden advance. She sat up straight as his hand reached her upper thigh. Leaning close in to her ear, he whispered, "Miss Sporty, can you take care of my little brother here? He ain't never been wit' no woman, so you gon' have to show him what to do."

His breath was hot and smelled like liquor. She was having such a good time with them she had forgotten that this was all part of the job. But when his hand inched higher and neared her crotch, she was soon reminded. Willy was shy and barely looked at her the whole time they talked. He was quiet, but he laughed at all his brother's bad, often vulgar jokes.

"You need to go see Miss Betty over at the desk," she told Henry.

He immediately jumped up and started toward the desk. Sarah was left sitting alone with Willy, who looked around the room rather than at her, his right leg pumping up and down uncontrollably from anxiety. When Henry left the table, Wallace came over and tugged at Sarah's arm.

"Let me talk to you a minute, baby," he said softly in her ear.

Sarah stood up, told Willy she would be right back, and walked with Wallace to the bar.

"Looks like you got your first one. You need to get on upstairs and get into that robe I gave you." Sarah saw from the serious expression on his face that he was all business. He was her boss, and it was time to go to work.

"Okay, WB. I'll go up right now."

"All right, and remember what I told you. If you need me, don't you hesitate. Hit that button, and I'll be up there."

"Okay."

Climbing the stairs, Sarah felt an intense rush, and her heart raced in her chest. She was shaken to her core. There was no more training left to do. No more pretending like it was all just a test. The time for turning back had expired. Facing the harshness of what she was about to do, she listened for any remaining guidance from Sister Anne or Head Mother, but their voices were silent.

"Lord, I pray I'm not making a mistake," she said the words to herself aloud when she got to the top step.

Still shaking, she opened the door to her room, thinking of Rita and Brady. Biting her bottom lip, she wondered what they would say if they could see her now.

I just need to focus on the money. I'll do this a few weeks, and then I'll be out of here.

Once inside, she took off the green dress, hung it in the closet, and put on the pink robe. She remembered last Friday when she and Rita talked to Shirley while she waited in her pink robe for her first customer of the night. It had only been seven days, but so much had happened it felt much longer.

Looking at herself in the mirror, she removed the butterfly clip and shook her sandy blond hair free so that it fell full and long to her shoulders. The sight of Iris, the man, and the whip flashed back at her again.

If she can make it look easy, it can't be that hard.

About that time, there was a timid knock on the door. She took a deep breath, stole one last look in the mirror, walked over, and opened it. There in the hallway was Willy, looking even more shy and unsure of himself than he had at the table. He stood there with his brown Stetson in his hand, looking at his shoes and not at her.

"Ughh, yes, ma'am" was all he could manage to say. So in the same way she had observed Shirley and Iris with their customers the night before, Sarah managed a smile, grabbed his hand, and pulled at him to come inside.

She led him over to the bed, where they both sat down on the edge, and she began pulling at the jacket of his suit for him to take it off. But she was still nervous and unsure of what to do or say, and so was Willy. He was the picture of awkwardness. She felt him trembling as she helped him slide his arm from the jacket. Unlike her first time with Wallace, she ended up doing all the work. She was surprised by how much Wallace had taught her and how oddly normal it felt being with this stranger. She touched him in all the places he had shown her that men like. She followed the rule and didn't kiss him on the lips. But just kissing him on the neck, his breathing grew heavy, louder, and rapid. When he seemed ready, Sarah reached over to grab a rubber from the drawer, but before she could get it, Willy let out a long high-pitched screech. The sound was like the noise a cat makes when someone accidentally steps on its tail. He fell back onto the bed, his body stiff and twitching. His eyes rolled back in his head.

He stayed like that for several minutes while Sarah waited for him to come around. When he finally stirred, he looked down at himself and then at her. Looking embarrassed, he stood quickly to his feet and pulled up his pants.

"Sorry, ma'am…that's all I need," he grumbled and hurriedly put his jacket on, got up, and went for the door. Before she could say or do anything, he was gone.

When realizing she had gotten through her first time with a customer, her first thought was, *That was easy.*

Chapter 12

Within minutes, Bobby was knocking at the door with clean white sheets and a towel.

"Here you go, Miss Sarah. Need anything else?" He eagerly handed her the folded white stack.

"Thank you, Bobby. No, I'm fine. I don't need anything," she said, unsure if that was the right answer.

"Okay then." He smiled, innocent and childlike, and was gone.

Soon after, Wallace stopped by to check on her.

"Everything all right in here, Sarah?" he asked when bursting through her closed door, concern on his face.

"I'm fine, WB," she said calmly but surprised by his sudden appearance. She pulled her robe tightly around herself, anxiously trying to cover a bare body he had already seen.

When he saw that she was okay, he grabbed and hugged her in a similar way a parent would do when a child they feared was in danger is found safe.

"Yes! That's my girl!" he said, grinning. "Now you let Miss Betty know when you're ready, and she'll send up the next one." He kissed her on top of the forehead and quickly left.

Sarah sat at the front of the bed, struggling to compose herself. Nothing much had really happened with shy Willy, but still, she was shaken by it. Willy was nice enough, but he was a complete stranger, and she had allowed herself to be intimate with him.

What would Rita think? What would Uncle Brady do? What would Sister Anne and Head Mother say?

She dropped her head to her chest as the look on all their faces revolved around in her brain. Reality had finally sunk in, and it was running cold through her body like ice.

I just need to pull myself together and stay focused on the money. It had become her mantra.

She shook her head like she was trying to clear out something that was confusing it. Breathing deep, in and out, she fought to get her nerves under control. It took some time, but eventually, she steadied herself.

I can do this.

In the same way she had observed the other girls, she went barefoot out into the hallway in her pink robe, caught the attention of Miss Betty, and raised her index finger to signal she was ready.

The next customer was a beet-red fortysomething man, who was particularly short in stature. When she opened the door and saw him standing there, he reminded her of an older version of the film star Mickey Rooney. If it weren't for his hefty protruding belly, the resemblance to the actor was uncanny. A gold band on his ring finger said it all.

For some reason, he was sweating profusely about the forehead and temples of his round balding head. It was so bad that the tan suit jacket he wore had perspiration circles around the armpits of both sleeves. The dank, sweaty smell of body odor immediately wafted to her nose. She couldn't help squinching her face when she looked at him, repulsed.

Reluctantly, she took his arm to pull him into the room, but he was quick to snatch it back, saying, "I paid for this, so I'll be in charge, little lady."

He followed her into the room without guidance.

Unlike Willy, he was aggressive and grabbed at her body deliberately and without reservation, yanking her hair and flipping her around like she was nothing. At one point, she panicked and nearly reached for the buzzer on the wall. The way he tossed her about reminded her of Shirley and how this must have been what it was like for her right before her customer started beating her in the face. Fortunately, when Sarah yelled, "No!" after the third time he slammed her down on the bed, he acted surprised at her outburst and calmed down.

The time with him seemed to go on forever, and she couldn't wait for it to be over. The more he sweat, the more the pungent smell of his body covered her and the room. The mix of perspiration and body heat made for an awful combination. The stench was a reminder of the way Brady smelled when he came home dirty and drenched after working a job in the sun all day.

When it finally ended, they were both wet. Sarah felt sick to her stomach and thought she might vomit.

Loretta was right; this wasn't anything like the way it was with WB. It was disgusting, and she felt dirty inside and out.

When he left, she froze against the back of the closed door. From across the room, she could see the full length of her pink-robed body in the mirror on the dresser. She stared long at herself, despondent, questioning who she was and how it happened that she ended up here—a sporting girl, selling herself for money. She barely recognized herself.

Who is that?

Someone older and more experienced had replaced the girl that had been there only hours before. This new person had the body and face of a stranger with contours and curves like Shirley, Iris, and the rest of them.

Is that me? She felt as though another person had invaded her body.

How could I have changed so much that quick? Everything is happening too fast.

In twenty-four hours, she had gone from being a virgin to a harlot. She was beyond rattled and didn't think she could handle another customer.

After Bobby dropped off his stack, she washed and scrubbed her body hard with water from the basin, trying to remove all traces of the hideousness that had just left. She took her time, combed her hair, put the green dress back on, and went downstairs. It was close to midnight, and the sound of swing was blaring. A few couples were dancing. It wasn't as crowded as it had been the previous night, but there were still about twenty people scattered around, drinking, talking, and enjoying themselves. When she found Wallace and began telling him about her experience with the wet Mickey Rooney look-alike, tears welled up and rolled down her cheeks. Seeing how upset she was, he quickly took her by the hand and led her down the back hallway to the supply room. When they were inside, he pulled her head to his chest, and she sobbed.

"He was disgusting! I just wanted him to get off me," she cried. "I didn't think I could be with another customer tonight, so I came downstairs. Are you mad at me?" She looked up at him, scared about what he would say.

"No, I'm not mad." There was the hint of a chuckle in his voice. "Most new girls have some kind of reaction after their first time. It's okay, Sarah. You did good. Did you remember everything I taught you? You used protection, right?"

"Yes, I did everything just the way you showed me." It made her feel better to know that what she was feeling was normal.

"Good girl." He held her close, first stroking her hair, and then moving his hand in soothing circles across her back.

"Sam could use some help, so why don't you go put on the uniform and help him until closing?"

"Okay, WB." She dabbed her eyes and wiped her nose with the white handkerchief he pulled from the breast pocket of his suit.

For the rest of the night, she was all over the downstairs, navigating her way around partygoers and serving the drinks Sam loaded onto her tray. Waitressing was easy and a big relief when compared with the job she did earlier in the evening. In the same way she had done the previous night, she kept a watchful eye on what was happening upstairs. Before the night ended, Iris and Loretta each had two more customers. One man Loretta had was drunk and could barely get up to her room. He made a spectacle of himself climbing the stairs while singing an unfamiliar tune that he struggled to remember the words to. When she came out in her robe, grabbed his hand, and pulled him in, Sarah could see the expression on Loretta's face when she saw the condition he was in. She looked the same way she had felt when she opened the door and saw the sweaty man standing there. Her heart sank to think of Loretta with a man so intoxicated and out of control.

Now that she was one of them, she empathized and understood the courage that was required to be alone and behind a closed door with a complete stranger. Anything could happen.

Chapter 13

On Sunday morning, Miss Betty made another big breakfast. This time, there were fried green apples to go along with the eggs, bacon, biscuits, and gravy. The aroma throughout the house was wonderfully powerful and delicious. It was 11:00 a.m., and everybody was seated around the table and fully dressed for the day. The small kitchen was cramped, but they all managed to sit fairly comfortably at the long oversized woodened table. The benched seating made it look like they were at a picnic as opposed to being inside having breakfast.

Iris, Loretta, and Ben sat on one side while Sam, Barbara, and Harry sat across from them. Wallace was in a chair that was pulled up to the head of the table; his attention was fully focused on devouring the food on the plate in front of him. Young Bobby ate hunched over his plate while sitting on a step stool that was pulled up to the counter near the stove where his mother, in a full white apron, was busy making another batch of eggs.

Sarah was the last to come downstairs. She was dressed in the clothes she wore on Friday when she arrived. When she stepped off the last step and onto the linoleum floor, she said an overamplified, "Good morning," to which no one replied.

Without prompting, Harry slid closer to Barbara to make room so she could sit down on the end and right next to Wallace. When she took her seat, Wallace looked up at her from his plate, grinned, and patted her on the thigh underneath the table. She was surprised by his show of affection but secretly loved it.

Within seconds after she sat down, Miss Betty was there with a full plate that had everything on it. Steam was still rising from the piping hot eggs when she put the plate in front of her. "Eat up now," she said.

"How was your first night, Snowflake?" Iris asked snidely from the other end of the table and so everyone could hear.

"It was fine," Sarah shortly responded, and kept her eyes on her plate.

"Sarah, you looked like a classy broad in that green dress last night!" Harry said, raising a forkful of eggs to his mouth.

"Sho' did!" grumbled Ben with his mouth full.

"A lot of men asked about you last night. That dress was working the room all by itself!" said Wallace.

The three of them all laughed together like they were privy to a joke only a man would understand.

"Wasn't no dress," blurted Iris. "It's 'cause she white!" She took an angry bite out of the biscuit in her hand and gave a bullheaded nod in Sarah's direction. "Loretta, you my friend, but these colored men like these white girls. This one here don't even have a good reason she need to be here." Iris pointed her fork at Sarah.

Everybody kept their attention on what was on their plates and ignored Iris. Her attitude and outbursts were clearly something they were all used to. There was an extended silence where the only sound was knives and forks scraping against plates and the occasional someone mumbling *ummm* in response to the tasty food. After a couple of minutes, Wallace finished eating, pushed his plate back, and broke the silence.

"Well, we had a good weekend. Everybody should be happy with what they got." He pulled a bunch of small white envelopes from his shirt pocket with each of their names scribbled on the front and handed them out. Sam, Harry, and Ben anxiously opened their envelopes and began counting the bills. The satisfied looks on their faces were proof they were happy with the contents. When he handed Loretta, Barbara, and Iris theirs, they each stuck the unopened envelope inside the neckline of their tops and into their bras. And each of them very matter-of-factly returned to eating their breakfasts. When he handed Sarah hers, she followed their example and did the same thing.

Once he handed out all the envelopes, Wallace left the kitchen through the side hallway without a word. Slowly, one by one, everyone got up from the table and said their goodbyes. Ben, Harry, and Sam lined up like children and paraded by Miss Betty, who was washing dishes at the sink. She turned her cheek up so they could kiss it but never took her hands out of the soapy water.

"See you next Friday, Miss Betty," Sam said when it was his turn.

Bobby looked up from his plate and took a high five from each of them when they passed by him. They also proceeded to come around the table and give goodbye hugs and kisses to Iris, Loretta, and Barbara. Sarah observed shyly, taking notice that they were all more than just coworkers. She was still seated at the table, finishing up what was left on her plate but stood up when she saw the three-man hug line headed in her direction.

"Welcome to the family, sis," Ben said when hugging her.

Harry embraced her similarly but whispered, "Welcome, Sarah."

Sam was last and added a kiss on the cheek to his hug. "See you next week, pretty girl." He embraced her warmly like someone would after having made a new friend. In the course of working with him over the two nights, the two of them had developed a connection. He was kind and thoughtful with a quiet, humble spirit, which made him easy to like. Along with Loretta, Sarah now also considered him a friend.

"I'm ready to leave for Warren whenever you are, Sarah," said Loretta as she put her empty plate on the stack of those on the counter to be washed. Iris and Barbara followed and did the same.

"Okay, I just need to go upstairs and get my suitcase."

Sarah stuffed the last biscuit in her mouth and watched as Loretta, Iris, and Barbara each went over and put their arms around Miss Betty, said their goodbyes, and left the kitchen. She looked longingly at how the cantankerous woman hugged each of them. After they were gone, Sarah got up and took her plate over and put it on the stack like the rest had done.

"I guess I'll see you next weekend, Miss Betty," she told her.

"All right, child, you take care of yourself now." Her Southern speak was delivered kindly as she continued wiping a soapy cloth across the plate in her hand. But she didn't look at Sarah or stop, wipe her hands, and give her a grandmotherly hug the way she did with Loretta, Barbara, and Iris. She didn't even tilt her cheek so she could kiss it, the way she did with Ben, Harry, and Sam. Feeling rejected but determined to make the mother of the house like her, Sarah spontaneously put both arms around Betty's shoulders and then cautiously but gently kissed her on the cheek.

"Thanks for everything, Miss Betty."

"You welcome, child. Now y'all run on so I can clean up this mess." Sarah didn't know if she made any headway with her or not but was encouraged that she hadn't pulled away when she hugged her.

Bobby finished eating and was helping his mother by clearing all the remaining dishes and utensils from the table.

"See you next week, Miss Sarah!" he shouted.

"You too, Bobby."

She ran up the back steps to her room.

When she got there and closed the door, she plopped down on the bed and pulled the white envelope from her shirt, excited to see what was in it.

"One, two, three." She counted the bills. "Four dollars!" It was more than she was expecting and definitely more money than she had ever earned and had at one time in her life. She held the four bills in both hands high above her head, staring at them in disbelief. She then remembered the dollar and thirty-five cents worth of change she had gotten in tips waiting on tables. Instantly, she was feeling better about everything. The dreadful things she had done with those two customers had been worth it. After all, the money was why she was there in the first place. Even the session with the stinky, sweaty man didn't seem quite as bad now that she had gotten paid.

I didn't even work upstairs the whole weekend! I wonder how much I would have right now if I had. I'll tell Uncle Brady I got a job waiting tables at a nice place in Youngstown. I'll give him two dollars and save the rest for New York. At this rate, I'll be out of here by August and forget any of this ever happened. I can't wait!

When she came downstairs, suitcase in hand, the house was still and quiet with a calm that was far from the energy that had filled it the night before. Loretta and Barbara were already outside in the car, waiting. Wallace was sitting at Miss Betty's desk, looking at some papers. Sarah wasn't sure if he was waiting for her or if he was just working. When she got to the bottom step, he got up quickly and came toward her.

"Didn't think I would let you leave without a proper goodbye, did you?" Before she could answer, he pulled her to him and gave her a kiss on the mouth that lasted several seconds. Not wanting to keep Loretta waiting, Sarah surrendered to him without even putting her suitcase down. It was unexpected and caught her completely by surprise. He hadn't acted like that since Saturday morning when afterward he said there could be no relationship between the two of them.

"I told you, you make me feel something like never before," he spoke in a whisper close to her face and held her by both shoulders.

"I don't know what I'm gonna do with you. One thing I do know, I'll be thinking 'bout you 'til I see you next week."

Sarah was stunned and didn't know what to say. She couldn't understand how much his attitude had changed since Saturday, but she was excited to see that it had.

"Okay, WB. I'll see you next week." She tried to hide how completely swept up she was in him.

Wallace released his hold and walked her to the door and opened it so she could leave.

"You're my special girl, remember that."

Dizzy from him, Sarah left, not knowing what to say.

On the way back to Warren, Barbara sat up front with Loretta. Sarah sat in the back and listened to their conversation as they chatted about the customers they had over the weekend. The drunk man that Loretta had been so disappointed to see when she opened the door had passed out on the bed ten minutes after he was in the room. She laughed, telling Barbara how it was the easiest three dollars of the

117

evening. Barbara had one customer that only wanted her to dance for him while he sat and watched.

"How about you, Sarah? Any interesting men this weekend?" Barbara asked.

"Well, I did have one that got me as a birthday present from his brother. He had never been with a girl before and was more nervous than I was."

Barbara and Loretta both laughed.

Sarah didn't really want to talk about it, though, or rehash the memory, so she provided few details. She definitely didn't want to relive her time with Mickey Rooney's look-alike. She figured Loretta and Barbara were also withholding specifics about the men they had been with. She was one of them now and realized there was so much more to the story about what happened once the door was closed and you were alone with a stranger. Despite the money and her refusal to admit it, the two encounters with the unknown men were still haunting. She did her best not to think about it. Rather than say more, she kept quiet and let the two of them talk. The rest of the drive home, she stared out the window at the crops growing in the fields and consumed her mind with thoughts of Wallace and what she was going to tell Brady.

Chapter 14

After Loretta dropped her off, Sarah burst through the front door like she was running from a fire. Her goal was to get to her room as quickly as possible without having to engage in small talk with Brady. When she came in, he was in his recliner, feet up, reading the *Sunday Chronicle*. He held it wide with both hands, completely concealing his face. He lowered it and looked up when he heard the door open. Four empty drink glasses were randomly sitting on the coffee table surrounded by unrecognizable remnants of food from something that had been eaten there. All were clues there had been other people in the house over the weekend.

"Hi, I'm back" was the greeting she gave when walking fast and doing her best to make an unsuspicious beeline to the stairs.

"Everything all right?" said Brady when he looked up with her rushing past his chair.

"Yes, everything is fine. I'm just tired," she said, respectful but grumpy.

"All right, well, I made some stew. It's there in the pot on the stove. Help yourself."

The aroma of the stew was filling the house. Brady refocused his attention and resumed his full-frontal position with his newspaper.

"Thanks, Uncle Brady, but I just need some sleep."

"Okay, Lucy Girl. It's in there if you want some."

"Thank you!" she bellowed, already halfway up the steps.

Lucky for her, talkative Brady didn't seem much in the mood for conversation either. Seeing the mess that was left in the front room, she figured he had his own weekend story that he just assumed not talk about, and she was grateful for that.

⤞⤝

It was the first Monday morning after the school year had ended. She got up at 7:30, put on black cropped pants and the white short-sleeve shirt with the word *Cashier* printed on it, and went to work. When she got there at 8:15, Mr. Fisher was already opening up and letting down the red cloth awning that hung over the front door. It had *Fisher Pharmacy* etched on it in bold white letters. After the awning was securely in place, he started bringing in the stacks of the *Chronicle* that had been dropped in front of the store earlier that morning. Sarah followed his lead and helped him bring in the papers. She was nervous to talk to him. But she needed to let him know she wouldn't be able to work weekends anymore because of the new job she'd started in Youngstown.

"You, young folks!" he said when she told him. "I knew when I hired you, a nice girl like you wouldn't be around for long."

He didn't seem mad, just disappointed. He also didn't ask any questions about her new job, and she gladly offered no details.

"Customers like you, Sarah, and I could certainly use the help, so if weekdays is the only time you can give me, then I guess I'll just have to take it."

"Thank you, Mr. Fisher!" She practically jumped with joy. The conversation had gone a lot easier than she expected.

At 12:30 p.m., she took her lunch break and walked down the street to Myra's Dress Shop to say hi to Rita. She was hoping Rita wasn't still mad and that their friendship could still be salvaged. The bells that hung on the back of the front door jingled when she walked in. Over the rows of tightly packed women's clothing, she could see Rita at an ironing board way in the back of the store.

Miss Myra was a pale but attractive middle-aged Caucasian woman who was known for her small-town fashion sense. It was an average Monday, but she was smartly attired in a navy-blue dress with a shiny gold belt at the waistline. All she needed was a hat and gloves, and her outfit would have been complete for a nice dinner in Youngstown or church on Sunday. Myra was at the checkout desk working and opening an envelope with a letter opener when Sarah walked in.

"Hi there, Sarah. It's been a while." Myra smiled and stopped what she was doing. She put both hands on her hips like she was eager to have a conversation.

"Hi, Miss Myra."

"How's your uncle?" she asked.

Myra and Brady had dated for a while, but it ended about six years ago. Everybody said they were a handsome couple, and it was expected they would get married. However, they broke up suddenly, and it was rumored Brady cheated on her with Miss Suzanne, the pretty brunette cashier at the A&P. It was a long time ago, and Brady didn't seem to like talking about it. Whenever asked, he would just say Myra wasn't the bride for him, and he showed little remorse about their relationship. But it remained his claim that Myra still wasn't over him.

"He's good. I'll tell him you asked about him. Is it okay if I say hi to Rita?" Sarah asked, pointing toward the back. Rita saw her when she came in but continued pressing the dress on the board in front of her.

"Sure, honey. Rita's in the back there ironing. Go on back."

When she approached her, Rita kept her eyes down on what she was doing. She didn't so much as look up to acknowledge a friend she had known her entire life.

"Hi, Rita. How are you?" Sarah approached her slowly.

"I'm fine," she said, pressing a very wrinkled blue polka-dot dress.

"I just stopped by to say hi. I've missed you!" Sarah stood there awkwardly next to the ironing board, waiting for Rita to show some sign that she felt the same.

Rita stopped, put the iron on its stand, put her hand on her hip, and looked at her. "Did you go back to that place?"

"I did," Sarah responded without hesitation. "Guess what? I made over five dollars!" She thought Rita would be just as excited as she was about the money.

"Well, I'm sure you earned every penny of it! I don't even want to know what you had to do to get it." Rita folded her arms over her body and loathingly turned her head in the opposite direction.

"Shhh, keep your voice down. I don't want Miss Myra to know," Sarah said, whispering.

"Pretty soon everybody is going to know. What will Sister Anne say? You won't be able to show your face anywhere in town."

Sarah swallowed hard, and her insides tightened at the mention of Sister Anne. Despite all the convincing she had done to make herself believe it was all about the money, a rush of guilt welled up inside her every time she thought about the Sisters and St. Bernadette's.

"Rita, you were the one person I was hoping would understand." Sarah leaned in but kept her voice down. "You know how bad I want to get out of this stupid town. I won't be doing it forever, just long enough to get the money I need to move to New York. Working at *520* on the weekends and at the pharmacy during the week, I'll have enough by August. Maybe we can both leave together, just like we talked about. What do you say?" Sarah pleaded, hoping they could still leave Warren together the way they planned.

Rita turned her attention away from Sarah and back to the dress on the board. She rotated it to a section that hadn't been touched and began ironing.

"I say you're not the person I thought you were." She stopped sharp and put the iron back on its stand again and stretched her head over the board toward her. "I've stood by you and all your crazy antics for as long as I can remember. But not this time! The Sarah I knew would never sell her soul for money. I don't want to be friends with you anymore if having sex with strange men is your idea of a plan to get out of this town." Rita frowned, looked down at the dress, and started pressing it again. "What will people think of me when they find out what you're doing, knowing we're friends?" she mumbled without looking up. "I think you should go."

"But, Rita—"

"Just leave, Sarah." She cut her off before she could make any further arguments to justify why what she was doing was okay.

Sarah left the shop in tears, her heart broken. The friendship she could always count on was clearly over, and it hurt. Rita was the one person she depended on to be there no matter what. She helped her keep both feet on the ground and out of the clouds the way Sister Anne always scolded her to do. Sometimes she listened to Rita's advice, and sometimes she didn't. But she worried about what could happen without the companionship of her levelheaded reasoning to help keep her out of trouble.

In the weeks that followed, Sarah focused on her two jobs and saving money. She told Brady she had gotten a waitressing job at a restaurant that just opened in Youngstown and that she would hitch a ride with two other girls that worked there. Every Friday at 6:00 p.m., she met Loretta and Barbara on Main Street in front of the bank. It was also where they dropped her off on Sunday afternoon around 3:00 p.m. She met them there in an attempt to avoid them running into Brady. Certainly, he would want to meet them, have a conversation, and ask questions. Loretta and Barbara were nice enough, but the way they dressed and their overly applied makeup would only create suspicion that they were more than just waitresses.

One Friday evening, on the way to *520*, they took a detour and stopped at a ladies' store on the east side of Youngstown, where Loretta and Barbara liked to shop. They helped Sarah pick out a few things: two colorful skirts with coordinated tops to match and a yellow party dress. Everything they picked for her was just like the attention-getting fitted styles they both wore.

"That dress was made for you, Sarah. You have to get it!" Barb said when she came out of the dressing room wearing the polyester A-line. It clung to every curve of her body and had a deep plunging neckline.

With coaching from Loretta, Sarah also learned how to expertly do her own makeup, the same way she had applied it for her that first night she worked upstairs. By mid-June, the pretty, naive young lady from St. Bernadette's had turned into a sensual vixen and a replica of the other working girls at the house.

She was making money too. She liked being able to give Brady a few dollars every Sunday night to help with the bills. He was impressed and kept saying he was going to surprise her and come by the restaurant in Youngstown to see where she was working. But so far, she had successfully managed to talk him out of it.

"Don't worry about coming, Uncle Brady. It's way on the other side of town. The food isn't that good. Plus, it's expensive," she told him.

Her relationship with Wallace also continued, even after he said he couldn't be with her in that way anymore. On Fridays following the regular 7:00 p.m. meetings, and sometimes on Saturday mornings, he routinely tapped on the door to her room for what he persisted in calling another one of their "training sessions." But their sessions were far from instructional, and more than once, their time together was so passionate he didn't stop to get the protection he had taught her never to forget. Afterward, his behavior was distant and emotionally repressed. He didn't speak and got up immediately from the bed as though he had performed some task on his list of things to do. He dressed quickly yet always paused for a second to kiss her on the forehead and tell her she was his *special girl* before leaving. Beyond the privacy of her room, he treated her like he did the rest of the girls. He was the boss, and they did whatever he said and without question. However, as the weekends came and went, there became no doubt in Sarah's mind that she was deeply in love with him.

By the end of June, it was apparent to everyone at the house that something more was going on between the two of them. Besides spending long periods up in her room, Wallace was overly concerned and cautious in making sure Sarah was okay. Harry and Ben were put on notice to keep a watchful eye on her room whenever she had a customer. And after each one left, he personally sprinted up to her room, just to check; something he didn't do for any of the other girls.

Shirley was well again and had returned. And with her back at the house, she and Iris were spreading all sorts of gossip. The two of them had the house buzzing with scandal about WB and "that white girl." It all came to a head one Sunday morning when Wallace was handing out the pay envelopes. When he handed Sarah hers, Iris piped up.

"I guess she got a little extra in her envelope, her being your girlfriend and everything."

"What are you talking about now, Iris?" said Wallace.

"We're not blind, WB. We see. We know what's going on between you and Snowflake."

Wallace stood up abruptly and pushed his chair hard into the head of the table, making a disturbing ruckus. He went and stood over Iris.

"First of all, Iris, you need to stay the hell out of my business." He looked down at her, putting his index finger on her forehead, and then pushing her head with it. "Second of all, what difference does it make to you anyway?"

Everyone around the table could see how angry he was, and it got eerily quiet. Seeing the intense scowl on his face and his massive body towering over her, Iris cowered and didn't say another word. Sarah put her head down but smiled to herself, watching Iris being put in her place.

Infuriated, with a grimace on his face, Wallace left the kitchen through the back hall. Immediately after, Iris gave her goodbyes and left out the back door. It was an uncomfortable scene. Even worse, it was now out in the open that something was going on between her and Wallace, and everyone knew it, including Miss Betty. Sarah knew she still wasn't one of Miss Betty's favorites, but recently, she thought she had made some progress with her. Now that it was suspected Wallace and she had a relationship, she worried about what to expect.

Later, when she was up in her room packing her things and getting ready to leave for home, Miss Betty pushed opened the door and walked in boldly while Sarah was sitting on the bed, counting her money. She was startled by her sudden entrance and how fast and aggressive she came toward her.

"You better take care, little girl," she said, pointing her finger in Sarah's face; she looked up at her from the bed. "That's a man you messing wit. You still a child. You best be careful. I seen other women mess up fooling 'round with Wallace. You sho' better be sho' you ain't one of them. You hear me?"

Sarah drew her head back in response to the finger in her face but didn't know what to say. Miss Betty put her face up close to hers and held it there for a second and stared. She was so close, in fact, that Sarah could smell the lingering scents of breakfast that rose from the white cooking apron she still wore.

Miss Betty made one of her deep-throated grunts then turned and left the room. Sarah was shocked by how forceful and direct she had been. It was almost like a mother correcting a daughter. However, in this case, Miss Betty was not her mother, and she was not the child who had to listen.

By the end of June, Sarah was a veteran sporty girl with dozens of customers of varying colors, shapes, and peculiarities under her belt. She was a facilitator of fantasies, many of which were perverse. But having been with so many men and carrying the burden of the dark, secret life she was living, the shameful weight of all of it was taking its toll. On Sunday nights after she got back home, she heated a huge pot of water on the stove and filled buckets that she carried back and forth and poured into a round metal number three bathing tub that was in the storage room off the kitchen. With the water as hot as she could stand it, she got in and sat down. She scrubbed every inch of her body with lye soap like a person obsessed, trying to remove all traces of the legion of strangers who had touched her. After a weekend of particularly vile characters, she would sit in the tub for a long time, scrubbing and scrubbing and trying hard to muffle the sound of her crying so Brady wouldn't hear. Later, lying in bed, her tears flowed silently when thinking about Sister Anne and Rita. The emptiness she felt inside was devastating and growing like a cancer. When reliving the last scene with Rita, the sting of her rejection still hurt. She was making the money she wanted but agonized about how disgusted people would be if they knew. She often thought of her mama and what she would say. No doubt, she would have been disappointed. Sarah knew Lucy would never have stooped so low—even if it meant she had to stay trapped in Warren her whole life.

"I'm not like you, Mama. I'll die if I stay here," she said in the darkness one night before falling asleep. "I'm sorry if you're disappointed in me."

Chapter 15

The next Saturday night, *520* was electric with the sounds of swing music and couples dancing. The main floor was bustling and tight with people. It was the weekend, and men were in their suits with money in their pockets, looking for a good time. It was almost 11:00, and by that time, Sarah had already had two customers and was preparing for a third. The first had been a lanky, handsome young soldier, excited to have just gotten home from the war. He talked about his girlfriend, Gloria, whom he was about to marry and how she had waited patiently for two years until he got back. Sarah could tell by the way his eyes sparkled when he talked about her that what they had was real love. He said he was there because he needed to sow the last of his "wild oats" before shutting down the store for good. He was careful and kind, and she was thankful for that.

Then there was the fiftysomething colored man. He was considerate but reeked from the horse stable he told her he had been cleaning that day. The suit jacket he wore was ragged around the collar, and his left pant leg had a nasty brown stain just below the knee; she noticed it when he tossed them on the floor. His insistence that she call him "poppa" throughout the session was creepy and more than enough to ignite the burn of shame that grew inside her. She did her best to ignore it.

Sarah washed with water from the basin, touched up her makeup, and came out of her room barefoot in her short pink robe to give Miss Betty the usual index finger signal, letting her know she was ready for the next customer. Just as she leaned over the top rail of the banister to try to get her attention, she got a shock like never before. On his way up the red-carpeted steps was Brady. The timing of both their movements was perfectly synced, and without even try-ing, they immediately locked eyes on one another. She panicked! Her first instinct was to run back to her room and hope he didn't recog-nize her, but there was no escaping that he had seen her.

"Sarah?" Brady yelled, loud. His face scrunched with amaze-ment and confusion, as if he couldn't believe what he was seeing.

"Uncle Brady!" she said, surprised and to herself. She didn't want him to see that she saw him. Her heart sank and raced at the same time, so she dashed back to her room and shut the door. Like a maniac, she paced back and forth in front of the bed, not knowing what to think or do. Within seconds, Brady pounded on the door with his fist while bursting through it.

"Oh my god, it is you!" He stopped in his tracks, stunned, peer-ing at her. "What the hell are you doing here, Sarah?" He grabbed her by both forearms and yelled, his eyes wide with disbelief. "I thought you were a waitress. Please don't tell me this is where you've been working all this time. Say you don't work here! Say it! Say!" He shook her violently as if trying to shake the words out of her he wanted to hear. Her body went limp. She didn't resist him. He shouted so close she could feel the heat of his breath on her face.

The sound of Brady's booming voice coming out of the open door of her room triggered security. Wallace and Ben rushed up the stairs and were there within seconds. Wallace came through the door first. When he saw how forceful and tight Brady was holding her, he grabbed him from behind, and they struggled. Finally, Wallace managed to pull him off her and hold his arms behind his back so he couldn't move.

"What's going on here?" Wallace asked, looking at Sarah.

Once free from Brady's hold, she folded over at the waste like someone in pain from a bad stomachache and wailed. Ben went and put his arm around her shoulder to try to console her.

"Let me go! That's my niece," said Brady.

"Your niece?" Wallace, still holding back Brady's arms, looked stunned at the back of his head, and then over his shoulder at Sarah.

"Yes, he's my uncle." She was crying, hysterical and could barely get the words out.

"I wanna know why she's here acting like a whore!" Brady lurched toward her when he said *whore*. Spit spewed from his mouth as he yelled. Wallace struggled to keep a hold of his arms.

Brady's eyes bulged through his glasses and were fixed on her. A huge vein she had never seen appeared on his forehead; it pulsed and looked tight. The sound in his voice came from a place she wasn't familiar with, and it was filled with rage. As mad as he was at Vernon that Saturday night he had tried to rape her, the anger he was displaying now was flamed by disappointment. She hated that he had found her there. Lots of times, she dreamed about what the moment might be like if he ever did. The humiliation she was feeling was even worse than the nightmares of her dreams.

"I'm sorry, Uncle Brady!" she sobbed, barely able to look at him. She was as devastated as he was angry.

Observing her condition, Wallace let go of Brady and went and put his arms around Sarah. She welcomed his embrace. Still crying, she buried her face in his chest.

"How could you, Sarah! Your mama wouldn't be able to look at you right now. She would be so hurt!"

Sarah couldn't come up with words for a response. He was the only father she had ever known. Since Lucy died, he had sacrificed and made sure she was taken care of. In return, she was repaying him by breaking his heart.

"Is this some of your doing?" Brady's attention shifted to Wallace. He pointed at him and then lunged, fist drawn, ready to throw a punch, but Ben stepped in between them and grabbed him by the shoulders.

"Hold on now, I don't want to get caught up in y'alls family business," said Wallace.

He let go of Sarah and stepped away from her. "She came here on her own. I don't force these girls to do nothing they don't wanna do."

"Did you know she was seventeen?" blurted Brady.

"Seventeen! You told me you were twenty-two." Wallace looked sternly at her.

All her lies were being exposed, and there was nothing she could say in defense.

"Uncle Brady, I never meant for you to find out," she cried. "You know how bad I want to leave Warren. I need money to do that. Mama couldn't leave because she didn't have the money. Uncle Brady, I can't let that happen to me!" Her voice was rhythmic with waves of high and low pitches. She searched for words to make him understand.

"This was just for a couple of months, and then I was going to stop."

Brady tried to compose himself. He took off his glasses, wiped his perspiring face with his hand, and then put them back on.

"I know you want to leave, but I would never have believed the little girl I helped raise would end up in a place like this, selling her body." He looked at her from top to bottom repeatedly. His shouting from before was replaced by more reserved tones, but his words were still emotionally charged.

"I did everything I could for you, Sarah. This is on you. I could see all the changes since you started working, what with all the makeup and the different clothes, but I *never* would have thought it was because you were a whore."

When he said that awful word a second time, the cadence of his voice changed yet again. This time, its rhythm was sadness.

"Uncle Brady, I'm sorry." She continued to cry.

Brady got eerily silent. He took his time, adjusted his tie, ran his hand through his hair, straightened his jacket from the skirmish, and walked toward the door. Before leaving, he stopped in the doorway and turned and looked back at her.

"I'm sorry, ma'am. I made a mistake. I thought you were my niece." He paused long, looking at her without speaking.

"Her name is Sarah. If you see her, tell her Uncle Brady is looking for her." He closed the door and left.

Sarah was shattered. Ben also left, but Wallace stayed behind to try to console her. She couldn't get the look on Brady's face out of her head. She had managed to control the emptiness that was devouring her by ignoring it. In her head, she was simply doing what was necessary to get to the world she thought was waiting. But when she saw the furious, mournful look on Brady's face, something inside her broke. Without fully realizing it, she had become numb to using her body as a tool for profit. Any consciousness she may previously have had for right and wrong had become distorted by the desire to live a life other than the one she had. She never really understood what Sister Anne meant when she insisted there was a little light that shines and lives in all of us. But right now, it felt like that mysterious little light had been extinguished, and her insides ached because of it.

"Are you gonna be okay?" Wallace handed her a handkerchief from the inside pocket of his suit as he sat with her on the side of the bed.

"I can't believe what just happened. Uncle Brady was the last person I wanted to see hurt by this." Sarah wiped at her eyes with the white cotton cloth and stared at the floor.

"You should have told me you were only seventeen. I could go to jail! Even worse, these white folks could kill me!"

"My birthday is soon, and like you told my uncle, you didn't force me to do anything I didn't want to do." She looked at him. Taking his hand, she squeezed it tight. "I love you, WB."

"You love me!" He stood up like a rocket and forcibly shook loose of the hold she had on his hand. "This was never about love. Is that what you thought? You're my special girl and all, but I ain't got time for no love!" he spoke plain and without affection.

His denial of any feelings for her was a crushing blow. Truth was, he had never said he cared about her, much less that he loved her, but she always hoped that he did. Normally, she would have known better than to utter words that said how she really felt about him. But something about the awful run-in with Brady and the feeling that she was now all alone in the world spontaneously forced her into confession.

Wallace went toward the door. "You can't work upstairs anymore until you're legal. If you want to stay on, you can waitress and help Sam."

"I want to stay," she responded shakily, trying not to let him see that he had just put a knife through her.

"Okay" was all he said, and he closed the door.

After he left, she sat on the side of the bed, staring at the floor.

Was that the right thing, telling him I want to stay? The wooden floor had her full attention. *I don't think I can go home.*

She wondered if Brady would even let her in the house. It horrified her to think of facing him again.

"What else can I do?" she said aloud. "I'm so close to having the money I need. How can I quit now?"

Besides, I'll be working downstairs with Sam.

Wallace had rejected having feelings for her a second time, but still, she couldn't bear the thought of not seeing him. She was hoping that he would have said he loved her too. That their time together had been about much more than just sex. As much as she wanted it to be that way, he had made it clear that was not the case.

Alone in the room, where she had been with more men than she wanted to remember, desolation and loneliness consumed her to the point where she felt physically ill. Still barefoot and in her pink robe, she pulled back the purple spread, got into bed, and turned the lamp off on the table. She curled up fetal, like a child, and pulled the cover over her head. The light from the hallway peeking through under the door was the only illumination in the room. The nightmarish scenes from the evening repeated in her mind as if on a reel. In the background, she heard the music downstairs and the stirring of the people. "Jumpin' Jive" was playing. The noises were those of intoxication and excitement. She was grateful for all the clamoring because she hoped it would drown out the sound of her crying.

Chapter 16

She was the last one to come down for breakfast on Sunday morning. Most of the night she tossed and turned, unable to sleep until about 4:30 a.m. when the house got quiet, and so did the chatter in her head. She woke to the aroma of bacon frying and biscuits baking. The smell was homey and provided a subtle sedative to the terrible night before. She opened her eyes but lay there motionless, staring up at the ceiling, quietly hoping it had all just been a bad dream. Slowly, she began to stir, but she felt disoriented and battered, like she'd taken a blow to the head. Yet the only discernable scar was the one on her heart. She sat up and reached for her mother's watch on the nightstand. It was 10:45, so she hurried and got dressed.

Coming down the back steps, she could hear the rumble of conversation coming from the kitchen. However, when she got to the bottom step and saw everyone seated around the table, the talking abruptly stopped, leaving her to assume she had been the topic of their conversation.

"Good morning," she said, reserved and not at all like her normal self.

No one spoke except Sam, who responded, cheerful as always. She took her assigned seat on the bench at the end of the table near Wallace. He never looked up from his plate as she sat down beside him. Everyone was quiet with their eyes on their food. The clanking of forks, knives, plates, and the occasional hum of someone enjoying their meal were the only sounds.

As usual, Miss Betty, in her apron, was quick on the spot with a serving of bacon, eggs, and two biscuits she had been keeping warm on the stove. She put it down in front of Sarah and went back to

134

whatever she was doing over at the sink. Wallace cleaned his plate, pushed his chair back from the table, and started distributing the envelopes.

"Loretta, Barbara, Iris." He handed them out one by one.

When he handed Sarah hers, the devious yet charming grin he usually gave her as their secret sign of affection was gone. When she didn't see it, the pain from his rejection came back hard.

"See you, everybody, next weekend," said Wallace callously and without expression. He left the kitchen through the back hall.

Ben and Harry also got up to leave, and the routine Sunday morning goodbyes were passed around.

"Okay, Miss Betty, I'll see you next weekend," said Iris when she hugged her around the neck. Before leaving out the back door, she looked at Sarah and frowned. She didn't say anything but rolled her eyes and made her typical disapproving hissing sound with her tongue. Bobby wobbled around the kitchen, helping his mother by clearing the dishes from the table and bringing them over to the sideboard, where she washed them in a tub. Loretta and Barbara were taking their time at the opposite end of the table and quietly going on about a john one of them had been with last night.

Sam told Bobby he was finished, and he took away his plate. Afterward, Sam slid down the bench beside Sarah. He touched her on the shoulder just as she was finishing her food and wiping her mouth with a napkin.

"Miss Sarah, we heard what happened last night. How you doing this morning?" His genuine concern made her eyes tear. And it confirmed that everyone in the house knew what happened. It had been the worst night of her life, but up to that point, no one had even asked if she was okay.

"I'm all right, Sam. Thank you for thinking about me." She put her opposite hand on top of where his was resting on her shoulder.

"I asked because I was thinking wit' all you been through, you might needed a hug." He opened his arms wide like a big brother welcoming the chance to try to stop a little sister from hurting. She didn't hesitate and fell into his chest. His arms were warm and secure around her and came at a time when she needed it most. She cried softly, not wanting the others to see. He held her long and tight and let her decide when it was time to let go. In the months that had come and gone, Sam had become more like a big brother.

"You gonna be all right," he said, patting her back. "Everybody have pain they go through. It's just your time. Lord don't never give us more than we can bear."

For a moment, she felt like everything would be okay just because he said so. She clung hard to his slender frame.

"We family. You need somethin', you can call on old Sam. You hear me?"

"Thank you, Sam." She held onto him a few more seconds and then let go, feeling a little better.

Up in her room, she packed to leave and thought about where she would go. In the past, whenever she had gotten into a jam or just didn't want to go home right away, she was always welcomed at Rita's house. But those days had passed, and that was no longer an option. She was getting anxious, not knowing what to do. She couldn't imagine going home and having to face Brady. Scared and frantic, she stuffed her clothes into her suitcase, not knowing where she would sleep that night.

What if he won't even open the door? What if he says he never wants to see me again? She couldn't bear the thought of another scene with him like the one last night.

Maybe Virdie will let me come stay with him and Aunt Rae?

Virdie was her cousin. He was in his late thirties and lived with and took care of his aging mother. Rae was Sarah's great-aunt. Aunt Rae and Sarah's grandmother, Francine, were sisters. Living in different towns and the differences in their ages kept Virdie and Sarah from being very close. The families tried to stay in touch, but they lived on a farm thirty miles outside Youngstown, in Ravenna. It was a nondescript little town even smaller than Warren.

It was only an hour or so drive that separated them, but traveling such a distance for a family visit meant planning and preparation. There were chores that had to be done, farm schedules to consider. Folks just didn't take a trip like that every day. Add to that, everybody in their family struggled to have enough money to pay for the basics.

A house full of company meant a big meal, which someone would have to pay for and prepare.

But Sarah and Virdie were family, and if there's one thing Ohioans believe in, it's faith and family! If she had no other options, she knew she could call him and he would do whatever he could to help her.

But I don't want to move from one stupid town to another!

"I may as well just find someplace in Warren to stay until I leave! Besides, I almost have enough money." She sat up straight on the bed and focused on all the money she had saved. She was only about ninety dollars short of her goal of four hundred dollars.

In a few weeks, I'll be on that bus that leaves Youngstown for Pittsburgh and then on to New York City! She raised her arms over her head and swayed back and forth, celebrating.

All this will be over soon, and I won't have to think about this place ever again!

Loretta and Barbara were waiting out front when Sarah came downstairs with her suitcase. On the ride back to Warren, she sat in the middle of the back seat so they could both hear as she filled in the details of what happened Saturday night. Recounting with them what happened with Brady was as horrible as she remembered. She avoided talking about Wallace and how he destroyed any hope she had that he was in love with her. Their relationship had been a secret, and even though it was clearly over, it seemed right to keep it that way.

"We heard you were only seventeen! Is that right?" Barb asked curiously, like she wanted an answer to a question that had been on everyone's mind.

Sarah was embarrassed when she reluctantly answered, "Yes."

Loretta held both hands tight on the steering wheel but took her eyes off the road for a second and looked at Barbara, shocked.

"Why didn't you tell us? I thought we were your friends, Sarah." Loretta asked, looking at her in the rearview mirror.

"I'm sorry. I didn't think WB would hire me if he knew I was seventeen."

"You're right about that!" she said, keeping her eyes on the road. "I bet he was mad as hell when he found out."

"That doesn't even begin to describe how mad he was," said Sarah.

They were all silent with their thoughts for about two miles when Sarah spoke up.

"I need somewhere to stay. I can't go home." Her voice was frantic. "Even if my uncle is willing to let me in, I'm not ready to face him. Do you know where I can get a room or something?"

"I guess you could stay with us until you find something." Loretta glanced quickly at Barbara to see if it was okay with her.

"I guess she could stay in the storage room off the kitchen. We would need to clean it out, though. It's small, but you could put a bed in there," said Barbara.

"Are you sure? Thank you so much!"

It's probably time I moved out of Uncle Brady's house anyway, Sarah thought.

They agreed that Sarah would come home with them, and the next day, while Brady was at work, they would go get her things.

The house Loretta and Barbara rented was cozy and cute. Sarah noticed as soon as she walked in the front door that they were particular housekeepers. Everything was tidy and in its place. The sofa and chair in the front room were Victorian and covered in a pink paisley fabric that nicely accented the mauve color on the walls. Behind the sofa was a three-level whatnot shelf that extended the full length of the couch and was dotted with carefully placed miniature pedigree dogs of different sizes.

"Those are my pets," joked Barbara as she pointed to the porcelain figurines.

The furniture and everything in the house had a newness about it that was welcoming, completely unlike the house she and Brady shared. Sarah couldn't remember the last time they bought anything new to put in the house.

The room off the kitchen was tiny, just like Barb said, and more like a big closet than a room. They were using it for storage, so it was filled with everything from a long rack with their winter clothes to sacks of potatoes and flour. But it had possibility and was more than adequate. Sarah spent a comfortable first night on the couch in their front room and dreamed lucid dreams of what her life would be like in New York.

The next morning, she called Mr. Fisher early and told him she was sick with a stomach bug and wouldn't be able to make it to the pharmacy that day. Barbara called her friend, Herman, who had a truck. Around noon, he showed up in his red Ford pickup, and the four of them went and quickly emptied her bedroom of most of her belongings. They loaded the truck in a little over an hour. She even took the bed, which she didn't really feel was hers to take, but she needed one and hoped Brady wouldn't mind. When the last of her things were on the truck, Loretta, Barbara, and Herman waited for her outside. Getting ready to leave through the kitchen with her arms full of the last clothes from her closet, she stopped and put them down across a chair. She found a piece of paper and a pencil in the junk drawer. Taking a seat at the kitchen table, where she had eaten countless meals her entire life, she wrote Brady a note.

Uncle Brady,

I'm sorry about everything. You've been nothing but good to me. I didn't want you to find out and hurt you this way. I'll be staying with some friends for a while. Please don't worry. I'll be safe, and I'll make sure they know how to reach you. I hope it was okay that I took the bed. I hope one day you'll be proud of me.
    I love you.

Sarah
Please pray for me.

She surprised herself when signing the note that way so much so that she pushed back from the table and stared at it. It seemed like such a grown-up thing to say: *pray for me*. More grown-up than she thought she would be to ever ask such a thing. Her brow furrowed looking at it. And she was strangely shaken by the spontaneity with which she had written it. Maybe it was the words staring bold back at her or the eerie silence of the mustard-colored kitchen in the busy house where she had lived since birth. But in that moment, she felt something big shift inside her and cry out. It was the first time in her life the words had real meaning, and she was stunned by the awareness of it. Her Saint Bernadette's education had taught her more than just reading and arithmetic; prayer was woven into everything they learned. In the quiet of the kitchen, she suddenly understood that. The light Sister Anne talked about seem to flicker a little inside her again. A chapter was closing, and another one was standing wide open, broad, and full of uncertainty. She had hopes for the future but no idea what she would face when she walked out the door.

Wallace wasn't in love with her, and the realization was a cutting pain. There was also her growing concern about her monthly, which was now officially late, something that rarely happened. In the past week, when she said her normal childlike prayers before falling asleep, she had begun adding something new to her well-practiced words. She asked God to please let her monthly friend show up soon! If that weren't enough, she had broken Brady's heart. The grimaced disappointment on his face was scarred into her memory. She didn't know when she would see him again, if ever. He was the connection to home and her mama. Leaving him was like leaving her.

She put the pencil down on the metal table next to the piece of paper and bundled the big mound of clothes back in her arms and got ready to leave. Standing there with the back door open, she looked long and inhaled deep, the small kitchen that still smelled of bacon and held memories of her mama cooking Saturday morning breakfast. The richness of it all was palatable. She could see Lucy at the stove and glimpses of her in every corner.

"I have to go live my life, Mama," she whispered to the stillness, hoping she might hear and understand. "I love you."

She closed the door and left.

Chapter 17

With some effort, Sarah turned the small storage room off the side of Loretta and Barbara's kitchen into a sanctuary. With their permission, she relocated and neatly stored the food, clothes, and other contents to one end of the small screened porch on the back of the house. The storage room was a narrow space that could only accommodate her bed and a side table. On the table, she put a few personal things along with a picture from Family Day, 1939, at St. Bernadette's. It was the annual May Day celebration. A day of games and fun for the kids and lots of good food bought by the parents. The group photo was part of the ritual. Second row on the right was Lucy, Brady, and her, standing next to each other, all smiling. It was the only picture she had of the three of them together, which made it special.

She thought carefully about how to maximize the tiny room and managed to store most of her clothes in boxes under the bed. Tucked into one of the boxes was the Maxwell House coffee can where she was stashing all her earnings. She covered it with sweaters for safekeeping. The rest of her clothes, she hung on hangers that were held up by two hooks on the back of the door. The room was so tight she could crawl onto the bed from the door. It was cramped, but it had a door and was comfortable.

The three women soon became family. Barbara was an amazing cook, and she made all the Southern dishes her mama had taught her. Helping Big Barb prepare dinner and cook for the big gatherings that took place at Loretta's family's home had proven to be an excellent classroom. Sarah didn't have any complaints about the five-dollar-a-week room and board she agreed to pay after tasting just one of Barb's home-cooked meals. However, she was aware that the added expense for room and board would slow down how fast she would be able to save money. August was within weeks, and she didn't want anything to delay her plan to head east. She had three hundred fifty-two dollars in the coffee can. Nevertheless, she felt safe with Loretta and Barb, and for the first time since she started working at *520*, she didn't have to pretend to be someone other than who she was.

Living with them also made getting back and forth to Youngstown easier. When she got home from the pharmacy on Friday, she had just over an hour to get ready to leave with them by six. Wallace announced to everyone at the next Friday night meeting that she would be working downstairs with Sam until further notice.

"We need Sarah here to help with the crowd downstairs," he said, pointing his finger across the room to where she was sitting. There was no reference to her age. But Sarah scanned the room while he was talking and could see from their unsurprised faces they knew the reason for the change. Iris kept her mouth closed but gave her usual eye roll the same way she always did whenever Sarah's name was mentioned.

She was happy to be working with Sam again. He was family, and fending off an occasional quick hand under the skirt the male customers sometimes tried to steal was nothing compared to what went on upstairs behind a closed door. The money wasn't nearly as good as she was making before, but she was glad to be waitressing again.

Her time upstairs and Wallace's teachings had made her artful at teasing and flirting. She used those skills while serving drinks with the customers to get bigger tips. A seductive stroke on the hand or a sensuous rub on a man's back while engaging in small talk could make the difference between twenty-five and fifty cents.

The second weekend she worked with Sam, she felt awful and spent most of Saturday night in the toilet out back heaving and throwing up. Her period had never been this late, and being sick to her stomach was an indicator of what she feared. The thought of being pregnant made her anxious, and the nausea even worse. No way she wanted a baby. A baby would ruin everything.

"You okay, Miss Sarah?" Sam asked when she came around the corner of the bar from her third trip down the back hallway.

"Yeah, I'm okay. But I think I have the flu."

She took a tray from the counter and began collecting empty glasses from the tables. She was still nauseous and exhausted beyond anything she had ever experienced. Wallace was at a nearby table talking with some of the customers but noticed when she came in from the back. He touched the shoulder of the bearded white gentleman he was talking to, excused himself from their conversation, and came over to the table she was clearing.

"You don't look so good. You all right?"

"I think I might have the flu."

"Well, then you don't need to be down here waiting on customers. Why don't you go upstairs and lie down? We're not that busy tonight, so Sam and I can manage down here."

"Thank you, WB," she accepted the invitation without hesitation. *At least he cares about me.*

If she was pregnant, she had no doubt that it was his baby. The constant insistence from both he and Miss Betty that they had to use rubbers was a house rule and one she had taken seriously and never broke. The only man she had been with without one was Wallace.

She couldn't wait to get up to her room. Kicking off her shoes, she immediately got into bed, fully dressed in her uniform and stockings. She fell into a deep sleep and had a dream that when she told Wallace about the baby, he grabbed her and swept her off her feet. It was a beautiful bright, warm day. She was wearing a white spring dress with a yellow ribbon around her hair. They swirled around and around while he hugged and kissed her about the face; he was so happy!

Her beautiful dream was interrupted when around 2:00 a.m. Miss Betty knocked on the door and walked in.

"Wake up, little girl. I need to talk to you," she spoke grouchily in her typical no-nonsense way.

Sarah jumped, startled, and turned over to see her hefty silhouette standing over her. The light from the hallway was the only thing illuminating the room. Groggy, she began to slowly sit up.

"Wallace say you sick. Is that right?"

"Yes, ma'am. I don't feel so good." She sat up straight, attentive in the bed.

"I came up here to check on you. You ain't gon' and got yourself pregnant, has you?"

"No, ma'am." She couldn't even imagine telling her the truth.

Miss Betty placed her open hand across Sarah's forehead.

"Most times, when a young girl gets sick to her stomach like this, it's a sign something else going on. You ain't got no temperature neither. So it ain't no flu. I don't know how many times we got to tell you girls to use them rubbers." Miss Betty stood like a statue looking over her in the dark with both hands on her wide hips.

Just then, Sarah felt a wave rise up from her stomach that she couldn't control. She leaped from the bed, pushing Miss Betty out of the way. She sprinted like a deer over to the washbasin on the dresser. Fumbling in the dark to find it, she vomited.

"Umm, hmm," Miss Betty moaned low and deep, watching Sarah heave.

"I'ma call Doc Southall and have him come take a look at you. If you is pregnant, we all got a problem."

The same snowy-looking, silver-haired gentleman who came the night Shirley got attacked arrived before breakfast on Sunday morning. Miss Betty brought him up to Sarah's room.

"Doc, this here is Sarah," she said when opening the door and once again walking in without knocking. Luckily, Sarah was already up. She tossed and turned most of the night, until finally around eight o'clock, she decided she might as well get up and get dressed. She had spent the past hour and a half sitting in the high-back chair next to the bed, staring into space, worrying about what she would do with a baby.

"Like I told you, she been throwing up but ain't got no fever."

"All right, Betty, let me take a look. I'll be down in a bit."

"All right then, Doc." She quickly left.

Sarah was thankful Miss Betty didn't stay while he examined her. He asked her to sit on the edge of the bed, and he pulled the high-back chair over and sat so he could face her. Locating a small flashlight in his black leather bag, he told her to open her mouth wide as he looked at her throat and then in both ears. He used his stethoscope to listen to her heart and asked her to pull up her blouse so he could listen around her stomach.

"Take slow deep breaths, in and out." Sarah inhaled and exhaled, following his instructions.

"What in the world is a girl like you doing at a place like this?" He let the stethoscope drop around his neck and looked over his round spectacles at her as he continued the examination. He felt up and down both sides of her throat with his fingers.

"What do you mean?"

Sarah kept her neck steady.

"Come on now…a young white girl in a house of prostitutes that mainly serves colored. You must have a good reason for being here." His voice was punctuated by curiosity and concern.

"I don't know," she said slowly, feeling embarrassed.

"It seemed like a good way to make a lot of money fast. I won't be here for long, though. I've got big plans, and they don't include Youngstown or Warren. I'm getting out of this place!" Remembering why she was there, the youthful tone of her voice elevated with conviction.

"You take it from an old man who has seen just about everything there is to see. The grass is not always greener. Sometimes young folks chase dreams that are not what the good Lord intended. You need to be extra careful what you wish for." He took his time, gathered the stethoscope, and put it back in his bag.

There was a subtle quality about him that permeated seasoned wealth. At nine thirty on a Sunday morning, he was in a tasteful three-piece suit. Even the care with which he removed his glasses, wiped them with a special cotton cloth, and carefully placed them in their case seem to translate his breeding. Sarah was immediately at ease with him, as though she was talking to a grandfather she never knew she had. He was friendly and wise and appeared to be genuinely concerned about her. The more they talked, the more she felt a connection with him. He spoke using words and phrases that were profound, and everything included a lesson. She couldn't help but pay attention.

"I've seen lots of youngsters get fed up with small-town life and head to the big city, thinking there's something better out there. I've also seen a lot of those same ones turn tale and run back here as fast as they could because it turned out not to be what they thought." He leaned forward toward her in his chair and placed his hand on top of hers.

"Young lady, I've traveled all over the world. Living in a big city is not for everybody. You can get swallowed up by it." He looked her straight in the eye.

Handing her a small cup with a lid on it, Doc told her he needed a urine sample. She got up and went over near the corner of the dresser where the night pot was, squatted, and filled the cup. Handing it back to him, he wrapped it securely in a white cloth and put it in his bag.

"We'll see what the rabbit has to say about this," he said, referring to the pregnancy test he would run.

"My mama wanted to leave Warren, but she couldn't put enough money together to do it. I'm not going to let that happen to me. Even if I do end up back here, at least I'll be able to say I didn't live my whole life dreaming about it. I have to go see for myself."

"Well then, I guess you have it all figured out," he responded, exasperated. Preparing to leave, he stood up and closed his bag.

"I just hate to see a pretty girl like you making choices that will haunt you for the rest of your life. There's a better way to do it, you know? An honest way. Don't be in such a hurry. You could ruin your life."

Sarah was silent; his words pierced through her. Ruining her life was definitely not part of the plan. But there was no mistaking she had done things that were unspeakable. All in a race to find a life, which, in truth, she really wasn't sure existed. That gnawing sensation inside her had become a constant. It was real. It had gotten worse every time another stranger knocked on her bedroom door and she opened it. When it was over, there was a deadening sense that less of herself remained. And even after a few weekends of only waitressing, that dark feeling was still there.

"I'll have your test results in a few days. I'll give you my number so you can call me." She watched as he wrote on his prescription pad and then handed it to her.

"Wallace's mother is my sister," he said, unsolicited while he was writing.

"I've been patching up girls in this house for years, as a favor to my nephew." Sarah was shocked to hear he and Wallace were related. She looked at him, eyes wide, and realized she didn't really know anything about the man whose baby she was carrying.

"Where did you think those eyes came from?" he joked. "Same eyes as his mother."

After Dr. Southall was gone, Sarah opted to avoid the judgmental looks of everyone at breakfast and didn't go down to the kitchen. Instead, she stayed in her room and waited for some sign that Loretta and Barb were ready to leave. She figured if she didn't show up, one of them would get her pay envelope. Her bag was packed, and the bed was made. She sat dressed in the chair, resting her head back to one side of it. Closing her eyes, she waited.

Please don't let me be pregnant.

Around 12:30 p.m., Wallace knocked on the door. "Sarah, can I come in?"

She jarred from her daydreaming and leaped out of the chair. Dotting over to the mirror on the dresser, she smoothed her hair down with both hands, straightened her blouse and walked over to the door.

"Hi, WB." She struggled not to show all the emotion she was feeling.

"Here's your money." He handed her the standard white envelope. "You doing all right? Miss Betty told me Doc Southall was up here this morning to see you."

"I'm fine. He's not sure what's wrong with me, so he's going to run some test." She did her best not to let him see how worried she was.

147

"You ain't pregnant, are you, Sarah?" He squinted his eyes at her.

She didn't know what to say, so she just stood there with her hand on the doorknob. She couldn't muster the courage to look at him, so her eyes drifted down toward the floor.

"You're no good to me pregnant," he spoke aggressively, and his tone showed the true nature of their relationship.

"Did you slip with one of the customers?"

"Slip!" Sarah shouted. She looked up at him, irritated. "I followed everything just like you and Miss Betty told me. You were the only one I didn't use a rubber with!" She leaned in toward him with a scowl on her face.

"Girl, what are you talking about? I know you're not trying to pin this on me!"

They were standing in the doorway, and Wallace's voice was increasing in volume, so Sarah pulled on his arm for him to come inside, and she shut the door.

"I don't want to be pregnant, WB," she said as calmly as she could. "If I am, everything I've dreamed about my whole life is going to be ruined. I can't let that happen!"

Her eyes teared at the thought of how much was at risk. Wallace calmed down when he saw a baby wasn't what she wanted either.

"Okay, don't worry. If you are pregnant, there's easy ways to deal with it."

She knew from the emotional void in his voice that he was talking about getting rid of it. "Doc knows what to do when this happens."

Regret pulled at her stomach. As scared as she was at the thought of being pregnant, to get rid of a child that was her own blood was overwhelming and more than she could process.

"He told me he was your uncle."

"Oh, he did, did he?" He smirked like he had heard a joke. "I guess that one caught you by surprise?"

"It did. But I always wondered how a Negro man could have eyes like yours." It was hard, but she managed a smile.

"So now you know." His response was guarded like a well-kept secret about himself had been discovered.

"He gave me his number to call him next week for the test results."

Wallace held her by the shoulders. "Don't you worry about nothing. I'll make sure everything is taken care of. This won't change neither one of our lives."

Sarah left the house in a daze that Sunday afternoon. July was almost over, and the air was thick and moist. She kept quiet on the back seat and looked out the window on the ride back to Warren while Loretta and Barb had their usual conversation, comparing notes on customers from the weekend. Listening to them talk, Sarah shook her head and wondered how this had become her life. How had it happened that her two new best friends were sporting girls? She would never have thought it possible. For the first time, she found herself longing for the life she had months ago, when Rita was still her best friend, when Brady still called her his "Lucy Girl," and the only worry she had was the absence of a plan on how to escape Warren. A baby might be coming, and as much as she didn't want one, she couldn't imagine getting rid of it. The get-out-of-Warren plan she had so confidently thought was her best option was now riddled with problems, and the money no longer seemed that important.

Falling asleep in her tiny storage room bed that night, she prayed, "Dear God, please don't let me be pregnant."

Chapter 18

Sarah woke up early on Wednesday morning and quickly remembered it was her birthday. Her long-awaited eighteenth birthday, which she had been so anxious to arrive, had finally come! She was officially an adult and could make her own decisions.

Lying flat on her back that morning, she gazed blankly up at the ceiling in her tiny room, in a bed she had slept in since she was nine. Her big day had come, but she wasn't nearly as excited as she had imagined she would be. It was the birthday she had waited for forever. That morning, she woke feeling like the coveted milestone had already passed, but there had been no recognition of it. There had been no party, no chocolate cake with white icing—her favorite, the one like her mama always made on her birthday. So much had happened; she was feeling much older than eighteen. Her face grimaced with the worries of an adult as she reflected on how much had changed since she left St. Bernadette's in the spring. Her long-awaited eighteenth birthday seemed insignificant when compared with everything else going on in her life.

After Lucy died, Brady put extra effort into making sure Sarah's birthday was special. He always gave her a few bucks, and then they would drive to Buckeye Diner in Akron for a birthday dinner. Nothing fancy, but they rarely ate out, which made it special. After dinner, the three waitresses that worked there would come out of the kitchen, singing "Happy Birthday," with a little yellow cake and a candle on top.

On the morning of her eighteenth year, she turned over in bed, her heart warm with memories of the way Brady grinned broadly, teeth showing, as the waitresses did their serenade. Until now, she hadn't noticed, but on this morning, she remembered that there had been a sparkle in his eyes when he looked at her from across the table as they sang to her. Year after year, it had been there—she just hadn't seen it before. Today she understood why the sparkle was there. It was because he was proud of her. She was his Lucy Girl. And after seeing the devastating disappointment on his face that night at *520*, the difference in the meaning of the two expressions was all too clear. She turned over in bed, the realization of it all piercing painfully in her stomach. She ached for her annual date with her uncle.

She turned over on her side and stared at the sunshine-colored wall. She took her finger and began drawing the outline of a cake. On top were eighteen imaginary candles. She could almost see them all lit up, just for her. For a few moments, she was transported and was imagining the birthday she always dreamed she would have. But just then, she felt the slow warm rush of something moving up from her stomach. She quickly threw back the cover, leaped to her feet, and rushed down the hall to the toilet.

❧

"It's your day, so just let me know what you want, and I'll fix it for you." Barbara was elated when she told her at breakfast that morning.

"I'll help too," said Loretta.

"Could we have the smothered fried chicken you make with mashed potatoes and green beans? Oh, and your rolls too!" Sarah inhaled deep and made an ummm sound, thinking about the incredible dinner they would have that night.

That evening, they ate on white porcelain plates with pink flowers around the edges.

"Barb, everything is so good!" Sarah said, reaching to fill her plate for a second time.

After dinner, the three of them were stuffed and sat around the table, laughing uproariously while they listened to Albert and Costello on the radio. After the show went off, Loretta took out three small glasses and filled her and Barbara's half full with bourbon.

"It's your birthday. We should toast."

"Yes, for sure, a toast!" Barb echoed. "A few of them sounds even better!" she said, laughing.

Loretta prepared to fill a third glass for Sarah when she quickly put her hand over the glass.

"Oh, no, I can't. Dinner has my stomach way too full," Sarah said but knowing that wasn't the real reason she refused the drink. Fortunately, they didn't question her decision.

They each took turns telling stories about the lives they had before the ones they were now living. Sarah talked about her lost friendship with Rita and how close they had been all through school. Barbara recalled about her and her mama picking beans together out in the garden behind Loretta's family's house.

"It was the middle of summer and hot as blazes!" She laughed hard when telling them.

"I wonder what my life would be like now if Daddy hadn't thrown me out that night?" said Loretta. "If Mother had believed me when I told her what he was doing to me and Barb!"

The sound of Loretta's voice changed quickly from happy to sad. She looked down at the white lace tablecloth and away from the two of them.

To change the downward turn the conversation had suddenly taken, Barb put Count Basie on the Victrola. The call of swing, ignited by the bourbon, was more than they could resist. They kicked off their shoes, pushed the plastic-covered Victorian sofa in the front room to the corner, and the three of them danced barefoot to the jitterbug.

Later, they sang happy birthday, and Sarah blew out a single candle on the chocolate cake with white icing Loretta made for her. Later that night, when she was nauseous and crouched on the floor with her head in the toilet, she had happy thoughts of their evening.

The next morning, she looked in her purse and found the wrinkled piece of paper with the phone number on it Dr. Southall gave her. While waiting for the operator to connect the call, she held her breath and braced for what she already knew he was going to say. When he said the test had come back positive and she was pregnant, it wasn't a surprise. But for the next two days, she walked around in a fog, unable to think clearly and conflicted about what to do.

"You look a little peaked, Sarah. You feeling all right?" Mr. Fisher asked Thursday morning when she helped him open the pharmacy and bring in the deliveries left at the back door.

"Yes, sir, I'm fine. Just tired," she told him.

Her despair was disorienting and sucking the life out of her. That evening when she got home from the pharmacy, she was exhausted and headed straight for her room. She had never felt more lost or alone in her life. It had been two days, and every minute of it, she wallowed in regret. She had made a mess of everything, and her well-intentioned plans were falling apart. Crouched in her little bed, she debated with herself all night whether to keep the baby or not. But every time she considered the extreme option of getting rid of the life inside her, the despair grew worst. The idea of adding one more terrible thing to a growing list of shameful choices was more than she could handle.

"Holy Mother of God, I need your help." It became her constant prayer. She desperately repeated it to herself throughout the day and all during the night as she tossed and turned, hoping she would have an answer soon.

In the car on the way to Youngstown that Friday, she shared the news with Loretta and Barbara.

"Do you know who the father is!" Loretta asked as she drove. Her eyes were wide with surprise. She looked at Sarah in the rearview mirror. Sarah thought for a second before she answered.

"I'm not sure," she said low and slid back in her seat.

If she announced that it was Wallace's baby, it would unleash a firestorm at the house. She didn't even want to imagine what Iris would say or do if she found out he was the father, so she decided to keep it a secret.

"What are you gonna do, Sarah?" Barb asked.

"What do you mean?" she was genuinely confused by the question.

"What do I mean...?" said Barb. "Are you going to have this baby or get rid of it? You're still young. This life we got is no place for a child."

"I don't know what I'm going to do yet," Sarah said abruptly. She didn't want to talk about it anymore and looked out the window, silent for the rest of the trip.

When they came through the door at *520* that evening, Wallace and Miss Betty were sitting at one of the tables in the parlor, talking and looking through the black book Betty maintained at the front desk. He stood to his feet immediately upon seeing them and took a manly flat-footed stance with both hands in his pants pockets. He was already dressed for the evening in a black suit jacket, white shirt, and black tie.

"Good, you're here. I need to talk to you in the back, Sarah." He was insistent and showed little expression.

Miss Betty didn't say anything but made her judgmental-sounding grunt. And she perched her lips tight as if to indicate she was privy to something that wasn't being said. By the looks of their faces, Sarah was quick to assume Wallace's uncle had already delivered the news.

"All right," she said and put down her suitcase.

"We'll see everybody at seven," said Loretta, and she and Barbara went up to their rooms.

Sarah followed Wallace as they walked around the bar and down the hall to the storage room. When they were inside, he pulled the chain in the ceiling and turned on the light. They found themselves facing each other in the same position they were on the night she and Rita were there, and he kissed her for the first time. She remembered that night when looking up at him. Standing so close, even now, she was overwhelmed by him in the same way she had been that night. He was the most handsome man, white or colored, she had ever seen, and his presence was intoxicating. Everything about him had excited her, and it still did.

"Doc Southall called and gave me your test results," he said matter-of-factly. "The rabbit died, so I guess we got a problem." There was a faint hint of his having made a joke, but she could see from his face that he was serious. "Don't you worry 'bout nothing, this can easily be fixed."

"I don't know what to say, WB." She dropped her head, unable to look at him.

He took his hand and pulled her chin up toward him. "You know what has to be done, right?" He held her jaw, his gaze on her steady.

"I don't know if I can do it, WB!"

"It's the only decision, Sarah!"

He took a few steps back and made gestures with his hands that signaled his agitation.

"I thought you said you had dreams? A baby would put an end to all that." He moved back in and grabbed her firmly by the shoulders to make his point.

"Don't you understand? This ain't nobody's child. This is just one of those things that happens sometimes in this business."

"I do have dreams…but to get rid of it…? I just don't know if I can."

There was a long pause as he stood looking at her, bewildered and irritated.

"Well, don't expect me to take care of this kid."

He started pacing back and forth in the cramped space.

"I can't believe I let you trap me like this!" he said in a frenzy.

"Trap you! Is that what you think I did?" She was angry and hurt. "I'm the one who's pregnant, WB! I could end up stuck in Warren for the rest of my life because of this!" She let go a flood of tears.

Wallace stopped his pacing, took her by the chin again, and got close in her face.

"If you decide to have this baby, don't tell nobody it's mine." His face scrunched and looked furious with rage. "I don't need these broads up in my business. You think Iris hates you now? You ain't seen nothing. So not a word, you hear me?"

She nervously nodded, shaken by the expression on his face. Letting go of her, he backed away. While looking intensely at her, he buttoned the jacket on his suit, straightened his tie, and pulled down on the cuffs of his white shirt on either sleeve. Once composed, he left the room and closed the door.

Sarah stood alone under the light, shaking and crying, stunned and devastated by his reaction. The fantasy dream she had that he would be happy to find out she was having his baby was just that—a dream. He wasn't going to take responsibility for the baby. If she decided to keep it, he wasn't going to be part of her life or the baby's.

He hates me now.

When it was clear that he wasn't coming back to say he was sorry for the way he acted, that he loved her and he truly was happy they were having a baby, she dropped to her knees, put her face in her hands, and sobbed uncontrollably.

Chapter 19

Waiting on tables and helping Sam with the bar was drudgery that weekend. She wasn't nearly as sick to her stomach; however, she was having a very hard time recovering from the gut-wrenching conversation with Wallace and his comment that she had trapped him.

How could he think such a thing! I trapped him? Why would I want to complicate my life with a baby right now? Frustration consumed her as she worked, delivering drinks to tables, picking up empties, keeping track of tabs. A steady stream of orders kept her busy and her tray heavy with glasses.

She also tried to avoid Wallace. When he came downstairs from his office to make his routine hourly security check and make sure everything was going okay, she was careful to look busy and not make eye contact with him. The replaying in her head of their conversation in the storage room had fueled her anger to the point where the mere thought of looking at him made her fume even more.

Miss Betty stayed at her desk all evening, managing what was going on upstairs. When one customer came down, Bobby immediately went up with fresh clean sheets and a towel. The first girl to lean over the banister and give Betty the single pointed finger got the next customer. Iris got one, then Shirley, then Loretta, and finally Barbara. And so it rotated. It was a typical Saturday night.

While going about her job in the parlor, Sarah regularly glanced over at Miss Betty, who was working at her desk. She was expecting that when there was a slowdown, she might wave her over to come to the desk for a talk or at least provide some sign or clue that she knew about the pregnancy, but she didn't do either. It was nearly 2:00 a.m., and she had yet to say a word about it. Even from across the foyer,

Sarah could tell that Betty was just her normal prickly self—fussing at Bobby, taking payments from men waiting to go upstairs, and generally behaving as though nothing was different.

By 2:30, the excitement and energy fueled by a downstairs full of people had simmered to a slow burn. Only three of the seven tables still had people sitting at them, and Sarah had cleared away everything on the remaining four. She took advantage of the calm to talk to Sam and tell him she was pregnant. Other than Loretta and Barb, he was the only other friend she had, and she didn't want him to hear the news from somebody else. When he didn't ask her anything about the father, she was relieved.

"It's gon' be all right, Miss Sarah," he said without much surprise. He was washing glasses in the tub behind the bar and lining the clean ones up to dry on the sideboard.

"I don't know, Sam," she told him with worry. "I'm eighteen years old, and I feel like my life is over before it even got started. I can't raise a kid!" The frustration in her voice was clear. "I barely know how to take care of myself!"

"Don't you worry none. The good Lord always has something else waiting 'round the corner. You just gotta hold on and pray. I made it through a war and two good-for-nothing women, so I know a thing or two about hard times. But as you can see, I'm still standing."

Sam kept his hands in the soapy water and looked at her grinning with his chest stuck out. He always managed to find the brighter side to any situation. Sarah loved that about him and even more now that she didn't know what to do and could use as much encouragement as she could get.

"The past few months, when I leave here after breakfast on Sunday morning, I stop by that little church up on the corner. You know, the white one with the steeple." He pointed his soapy finger toward that direction.

"You mean the one with the bell that wakes me up every Sunday?" she joked, remembering how jarring the clanking bell was that woke her from a deep sleep. As loud as it was, she found it oddly comforting, like a welcome sign that she had survived a night of dark secrets.

"Maybe you should come wit' me tomorrow. The preacher there always gives you a good word to feed your soul. It's helped me a lot. Maybe it'll help you too."

"Okay, maybe I will go with you, Sam." She was encouraged at the idea. "Oh, but I can't miss my ride back to Warren with Loretta and Barb."

"Well, maybe they should come too," he said.

When most of the customers had gone, Loretta and Barb came down to relax, unwind, and get their nightcaps. Sarah shared Sam's invitation with them, and to her surprise, they immediately said they wanted to come along.

"We all could stand to go to church," said Loretta. "I haven't been since I left home, but it's something I've been meaning to do. As controlling a devil as he was, my daddy made sure my mother, my brothers, and me were present at the Presbyterian church every Sunday morning, looking like the perfect family. What a lie that was."

"Yeah, I need to go too," said Barb. "If Big Barb knew how long it's been since I stepped foot inside a church, she would have my behind."

While they were talking and laughing, Iris came down and went and sat alone at a corner table without so much as a nod to acknowledge they were there. She put a cigarette to her lips, lit it with a match, and appeared to be very content sitting by herself. Sam went over with a glass and a bottle and poured her a drink. Within a few minutes, the final customer of the night was coming down the stairs from Shirley's room, his plaid suit jacket draped over one arm. There was the hint of a smile on his ebony face as he adjusted his tie. And the wide-legged peacock gate in his step seemed to suggest he was satisfied.

"Y'all have a good night now," he said, tipping the brim of his fedora at them as he exited out the front door.

Realizing all the customers were gone, Loretta piped up across the room to get Iris's attention.

"Hey, Iris, we're all going to church tomorrow morning. Do you want to come?"

"Church! Y'all must be crazy," she said, mocking them. She took a sip of her drink and another long drag of her cigarette, releasing a plume of smoke.

"That church might catch on fire when the three of y'all walk through the doors." She laughed.

"Sam is going too," Loretta added.

"Well, at least he can help put out the flames. No, thank you," she blurted. "Count me out."

"I guess it's just us four," said Barbara, turning her attention back to the three of them.

Miss Betty was still at the desk but finished and came over to their table. "Did I hear y'all say something about going to church?"

"Yes, ma'am, we're going in the morning," said Loretta.

"Lord have mercy," she said in her Southern drawl. She bent over laughing. "I hope dim folks are ready for the likes of you three!" She laughed hard again and covered her mouth with her hand, like she didn't want anybody to see her teeth. It was the first time Sarah had ever seen her laugh. It was a nice break from her normal scowl. But she was disappointed that the first time she got to see the lighter side of the snarly old woman, it came at their expense. Responding to Miss Betty's laughter, Iris chimed in from the corner.

"Miss Betty, I told them they ain't got no business in no church," she said loudly, and the two of them laughed and laughed.

On Sunday morning, Loretta and Barb were dressed and eating breakfast with Ben, Harry, and Sam when Sarah came down and joined them at ten thirty. Miraculously, they had transformed themselves from the attention-getting seductresses they normally were into demure, ladylike women. Both wore little makeup and had pulled back their hair into a matronly bun. They looked more like conscientious schoolteachers than sporting girls. Barbara had on a simple green cardigan sweater, but instead of leaving it partially unbuttoned the way she normally did, displaying her cleavage, the knit fabric was buttoned up to her neck. When Sarah saw the two of them seated at the breakfast table looking strangely normal, she couldn't help but grin. She had also dressed respectfully, not wanting to draw too much attention. Like them, she dressed simply in a navy-blue skirt and plain white blouse. The three of them were a curious trio, but they had done a good job of masking who they really were.

"Good morning everybody," Sarah said quietly, taking a seat on the bench next to Sam.

"Good morning," they collectively grumbled.

Miss Betty brought her a plate with country sausage, scrambled eggs, and two biscuits, which she had been keeping warm for her on the stove. Sarah was routinely the last one down for breakfast, so Miss Betty always kept a plate warm for her. It was one of the few real acts of kindness the woman ever showed her. Wallace's chair at the head of the table was pulled up close like he had never been there, or perhaps he had eaten his breakfast earlier and had long since gone. At any rate, Sarah was glad to have avoided him yet again. There were a few envelopes laid out on the table where his plate would have been. Sarah saw her name on one, so she reached over and got it and stuffed it in her shirt.

"Miss Loretta, why don't you leave your car here and we can all walk up the street to the church?" Sam said as he took the last bites of his food.

"All right. Do you think the people there will be okay with the sight of us? We don't exactly look like typical churchgoers."

"Nah, the people there don't care nothing 'bout what you look like, long as you there to praise the Lord."

"Y'all are really going to church?" Ben asked, in disbelief.

"Yep, you can come wit' us if you want," Sam told him.

"Nah, that's okay. Say a prayer for me, though." The tone of his voice was a mix of humor and sincerity.

"Say one for me too," said Harry.

They walked up the street in the bright warm sun of a summer morning with the birds chirping. When they got to the steps of Livingston Street Church of God, they could hear a piano playing and the choir singing "What a friend we have in Jesus, all our sins and griefs to bear. / What a privilege it is to carry, everything to God in prayer."

"Y'all ready?" Sam said, looking at the three of them.

He got no response. They were focused on the closed wooden door in front of them and clearly nervous about what waited on the other side. Loretta and Sarah were both white with fear, and Barbara was reserved and intent. Sam opened the door, and they walked in. The congregation was standing and singing along with the six people—four women and two men—who were in the choir box behind the pulpit. A white-gloved, colored male usher directed them to an empty pew on the last row of the small packed church. Sarah walked close behind Sam; Loretta and Barbara followed.

When the song ended and everyone took their seats, the preacher, Reverend Abraham Wright, a stately gray-haired dark man in a black robe approached the podium and prepared to speak. The expression on his face was serious. He took his time and flipped through the pages of the Bible. The gathering of parishioners whom only moments before had been so gleeful with song was now quiet and waiting. There was collective anticipation about what the reverend would have to say.

"Can the church say amen?" he told the congregation in his deep voice.

In unison, they responded, "Amen."

And then he began to preach.

"Church! I came here to tell you today that the Lord is moving in here this morning." He paused and looked around at the congregation as though he was searching.

"Somebody in here needs Jesus!" The reverend stretched his robed arm out long and moved his pointed finger back and forth across the congregation. He peered with intention over his horn-rimmed glasses, seemingly looking to find anyone to whom he might be speaking.

"The Word says, seek and you will find, knock and the door will be opened unto you. Somebody in here is seeking answers to questions only Jesus can answer! I'm telling you, He's moving in here this morning, church!"

When he said "He's moving" a second time, the reverend jumped straight up, came down, and hit the Bible hard in the center with his fist. He then did a 360-degree turn on the heel of his right shoe. The congregation reacted with excitement, and many of them stood to their feet and repeatedly shouted, "Amen! Amen!"

A few of the older ladies held up white handkerchiefs and waved them in the air in a symbolic gesture of being in agreement with everything he said.

Sarah had never experienced a church like this before. She sat frozen in her seat, both shocked and mesmerized. It was nothing like the masses at St. Bernadette's Church, where the congregants sat quiet and stoic, listening to the priest calmly deliver his message. Reverend Wright's high energy and the participation by the congregation were all so wonderfully different. She was moved by it. A chilling rush flowed through her body.

"I don't know who in here needs a Word this morning, but the Lord sent me here to tell you that you need to come home. If you're hurting and sad, come home. If you've lost your way, come home. He'll be the Father you never had. He wants to take care of his child. So come on home to Him!"

Sarah clung to his every word, concentrating on all that he said. She was so captivated, in fact, that she began feeling like everyone else in the church had faded away, and she was the only one he was speaking to. At one point, she actually thought he called her by name.

As he preached, her life played out like a movie at the fringes of her mind. The future she wanted, and all she had sacrificed to get it, had been for nothing. Everything was slipping away, and she was helpless to stop it. Her escape plan, that she had been so confident about, had backfired, and the consequences were devastating. A baby was growing inside her. She could barely afford to take care of herself, let alone a baby. What kind of life could she give it? Because *520* was no place to raise a child, and it had been so long since she saw Uncle Brady...there was no way she could show up on his doorstep, pregnant and asking to come home. Loretta and Barb might let her continue to stay with them, but their place was tiny and cramped. And she couldn't count on WB. He made it clear he didn't want anything to do with her or their baby. There were no options that made sense. The more she agonized about her circumstances, the greater the hopelessness in her heart became. Tears came easy.

Sitting beside her on the pew, Sam saw she was crying. He put his arm around her shoulder and pulled a handkerchief from his pocket and handed it to her. Loretta and Barb were composed, but both sat up straight and attentive in their seats, engrossed in all that was being said. When Reverend Wright talked about Jesus and the leper, Barbara reached over and grabbed her adopted sister's hand from her lap and squeezed it.

"The Father knows everything you've done. He was there. He saw it! Still, he loves you unconditionally. You can be made whole again! He's saying, come on home to me, [*Sarah*]. I'm here to help you. My yoke is easy, and my burdens are light."

Again, Sarah thought she heard him call her name.

The reverend spoke about forgiveness. "No matter what you did, God loves and forgives you."

Could God really love me after all the terrible things I've done? All the people I've hurt and disappointed? She felt so unworthy.

But as he preached, a new sense of clarity came over her like a wave and sent a euphoric sensation throughout her body. It brought with it an acute awareness of how she had tossed aside everyone who loved her in a desperate chase to find a dream that might not even be real. She had completely disregarded everything the sisters taught her in school, and now, as a result, she was paying the price.

Uncle Brady and Rita loved me, and I ruined everything!

Reverend Wright's words made her realize the heavy burden of regret she had been carrying. For months, she had been trying hard to ignore the dark feeling that was always present. But the emptiness still consumed her.

It was painful for her to look at her life and come to see that she had to take ownership of the consequences that resulted from her bad decisions. As cutting to her spirit as his message was, his sermon was strangely filling her with hope. As he continued preaching, she began to feel lighter, like a huge weight had been strapped to her back, and finally, she was able to put it down for a moment and rest. She was clueless about what was ahead for her. Yet for the first time in a long time, she had an unexplainable sense of peace at the end of his sermon, like everything was going to be all right.

After the service, Reverend Wright stood at the door of the church, shaking hands with the people as they were leaving. When it was Sarah's turn, she shook his hand then instinctively put her arms around his huge frame, hugging him around the neck.

"Thank you for your sermon today, Reverend," she said quietly in his ear.

"It's going to be all right, child," he whispered. He returned the hug she was in desperate need of. "Jesus loves you," he told her. "If you ever want to talk about it, come by the church anytime. I'm here most days."

"Thank you, Reverend. I'll remember that."

The three young women had a quiet ride back to Warren that afternoon. Reverend Wright had given each of them a lot to think about, and it was preoccupying their thoughts. Barbara could be heard sniffling from time to time. She didn't talk and kept her eyes out the window and onto the cornfields they passed along the road. Loretta was mindful of the highway but used the car door to support her left elbow so she could massage the furrowed worry lines of her forehead. The two of them had their own demons to deal with. Neither had seen their families in over ten years, and if they were to see them now, there was nothing either of them could say about their lives to make them proud.

The reverend's message made an impact on Sarah. She left church that day, knowing she was keeping the baby.

It's not what I wanted, but I'm responsible for this baby and the choices I made that created it.

She knew she would have to accept that her plan would have to change. It couldn't just be about her anymore…she would need a new plan. One that included the baby.

Chapter **20**

The next weekend, Miss Betty came to her room on Friday night just as she was putting her weekend clothes away in the bureau.

"Little girl, I know what's going on wit' you," she said when walking in unannounced. It was unexpected, and Sarah was startled at her sudden entrance.

"Ma'am?" she said, turning around quickly to see her already standing right in front of her.

"No need to act dumb wit' me. You know what I'm talking 'bout. You done gone and got yourself pregnant, just like I thought."

"Yes, ma'am," Sarah said, lowering her head in shame and resumed putting the last of her clothes in the drawer. There was little else she could think to say. To add the missing detail that it was Wallace's baby would probably just make things worse.

"Lord, have mercy, it's Anna all over again!" Betty stood with both hands on her wide hips with a scowl on her face that was even more fearsome than usual.

"I talked to Wallace, and he wants you to help Sam from now on. But I already told him it won't be for long. These men ain't gon' want to be waited on by a girl with a big belly. We just gon' have to see."

The news of her pregnancy eventually made its way to everyone in the house. One Saturday night before she began showing, Iris let it be known that she and Shirley knew her secret as they sat having their after-closing drink. Sarah was busy with the normal cleanup, collecting glasses on a tray and wiping down the tables.

"So, Snowflake, we hear you gone and got yourself caught," Iris barked at her from a nearby table.

"What?" Sarah responded, both caught off guard by the comment and annoyed by it.

"Everybody here knows you pregnant, so you can stop puttin' on and acting like you're not."

"I'm not acting! I just didn't think I needed to announce it." Sarah focused on wiping down the table she had just cleared and tried not to get distracted by Iris's bullying.

"You ain't gonna be able to hide it but for long, Sarah," said Shirley.

Unlike Iris, Shirley was more empathetic, less confrontational, even understanding. Sarah remembered the story she told her and Rita the night they met, about what happened to Anna. The awful scene the night she gave birth and how the baby was snatched away.

⊱⊰

By February, her stomach had grown large, and there was no mistaking that she was pregnant. Serving drinks and helping Sam was her full-time occupation. The money was a fraction of what she made upstairs, and she noticed the larger she got, the smaller the tips became. Flirting with the men to get them to leave bigger tips felt awkward once she started showing, and she soon saw the difference in her money.

She quit her job at the pharmacy right after Dr. Southall confirmed she was pregnant. The last thing she wanted was it getting around town that she was not married and having a baby. The money from waitressing wasn't much, but it paid for room and board, and there was still a little leftover to put in her coffee can bank. Having a normal job, although at a brothel, made her less contemptuous about herself, and little by little, she was regaining dignity.

The earlier relationship she had with Wallace when she was his "special girl" changed completely, and she was demoted to being just one of the other females at the house. The only difference was she was the only one with a swollen belly. To his credit, Wallace did inquire with her regularly about how she was feeling, and he was quick to tell her to go upstairs and lie down for a while if he thought she looked tired.

"Don't worry 'bout nothing down here. Sam and me can handle it," he would say.

She knew he didn't love her, but when he acted caring and kind that way, she was reminded that she still loved him.

Since their first Sunday church service together, Sam, Sarah, Loretta, and Barb went back to the little church up the street several more times. Sarah looked forward to the reassuring hug Reverend Wright gave her at the end of the service. At his invitation, she nervously went by the church to see him one Saturday morning after breakfast. He heard the creak of the front door open and came out of a side room just off the pulpit to see who it was. When she saw him, her heart raced. The black robe-draped image she had of him was replaced by a sixtysomething man in plain trousers and an open-collar white shirt. He appeared unusually normal without the clothing of the pulpit. However, the robe had not disguised the fact that he was large in stature. He had a prominent presence, even in street clothes. She was intimidated by being alone with such a powerful man of God, whom she had grown to admire and respect.

"Well, hello there. Come on in, child."

Recognizing who she was, he waved his hand and beckoned her to come up to the front. Frightened, she walked up to meet him. They met right in front of the communion table.

"I was working on my sermon for tomorrow. 'You're Never Alone' will be my subject," he said, clearly excited about the topic.

"Let's sit down here for a spell and talk." He pointed to the first pew. A large cross with Jesus hung on the wall behind the pulpit. Seated in the back, where they always sat with the church packed with people, the cross had seemed far away. But sitting now at the front and so close, it appeared huge. In the quiet of the sanctuary, Sarah felt a humbling sense of power emanating from it.

She and the Reverend Wright talked for over an hour. She confessed all the bad choices she'd made while attempting to find the life she always dreamed about. How it had all resulted in her being pregnant by a man she loved but who didn't love her. When she talked about Wallace and the baby, her heart filled to the brim, and it made it difficult for her to speak.

"Reverend, I've made such a mess of my life," she said, her voice shaking. "What started out as my plan to escape to a better life has turned into a prison. And I don't know how to get out of. I don't know what to do!"

She went on to tell him how she had disappointed the two people she loved most in the world. Desperation was on her face and in her voice when she put her head in her hands and began sobbing. The reverend pulled out his handkerchief and handed it to her. He placed his hand on her shoulder and looked at her sternly.

"Listen to me, my daughter, the Lord God is full of forgiveness and mercy. Nothing you have done can stop Him from loving you. You need to understand that." The reverend grew more serious. He squinted his eyes when making his point. "He is the best friend you will ever have, and He will never leave you alone. You can trust Him to help see you through everything you're worried about." He gently squeezed the hand that was on her shoulder. "But you have to know Him for yourself." Reverend Wright got up from the pew and went into the room off to the side of the pulpit. When he came out, he held a small brown leather Bible in his hand. He handed it to her.

"Take this. Everything you need to know is in this book."

"Thank you, Reverend." She managed a smile and accepted the gift.

He took her hand and beckoned for her to stand to her feet. There, in front of the communion table and the cross, he told her to close her eyes. He laid his huge hand on her head and began to pray.

"Lord, bless this young woman, Sarah, who has come here seeking guidance. Lord, she is Your child, and she's lost her way. Speak to her heart, God, as only You can, and let her know everything will be all right if she will only trust and believe in You. Bless the child she's carrying. May it grow to be healthy and strong and become a bright light in this world..."

By the time the reverend finished praying, he had covered every challenge Sarah was facing in her life. He even asked God to restore the broken relationship with her uncle, to which she openly responded, "Please, God!"

Chapter 21

On a frigid cold Friday night in late February, the evening was off to a slow start. It snowed hard earlier that week, but it had hardly melted because of the freezing temperatures. Everybody at the house was expecting it to be a slow night because of the weather. But by 8:30, there were four men in the parlor and two upstairs. Sam put Frank Sinatra's "Night and Day" on the Victrola, creating an atmosphere downstairs that was relaxed and mellow. When the front door of the foyer opened, Sarah looked up from her serving tray to see who appeared to be her cousin, Virdie. She squinted her eyes in an attempt to confirm if it was him. He was by himself, and based on the lost look on his face, he wasn't quite sure where he was. Sarah hadn't seen him in over a year when he was at the house one Saturday night playing cards with Brady and some of his friends.

When she realized it was Virdie, Sarah put down her serving tray and went over to where he was standing on the landing. He looked underdressed, out of place, and confused. Acceptable customer attire at 520 was, at a minimum, well-groomed and gentlemanly. Virdie's parka coat atop bib overalls made him stand out like a spotlight.

"Virdie?" she said, questioningly, when she approached him.

"Sarah!" He looked at her with disbelief. "Uncle Brady said you would be here. He sent me to check on you. What the hell are you doing in this place?" He rotated his head in different directions, scanning the surroundings in amazement like a pioneer in new territory.

"This is where I work," she responded, sheepish.

Though he was nearly twenty years older than her, rural farm life in Ravenna had not prepared Virdie for the rest of the world. Planting and harvest were the big news topics where he came from.

170

His experience was limited, and it showed in the way he dressed, the uneducated way he talked, and everything else about him.

"Are you pregnant!" he said with his mouth hanging open and looking at her swollen stomach.

"Yes, I'm having a baby." Embarrassed, she put her index finger to her lips to let him know he was talking too loud.

"Uncle Brady doesn't know, does he? This is going to kill him for sure!" Virdie looked at her with his eyes wide and pressed an open hand against the side of his head, showing his shock.

"Who's the father?" he asked. She didn't answer him.

"We need to talk, Virdie," she whispered. "Come on in and let me get you a drink." Sarah took his hat and coat and put it on the rack. She grabbed his forearm as if leading someone blindly and guided him to one of the empty tables.

"Sit here, and I'll bring you a shot of whiskey."

Virdie sat and waited pensively for Sarah's return. He was pale like a ghost and gazed curiously around the room. The turned-up corners of his tightly closed thin lips showed his disapproval with everyone and everything he saw. By the time Sarah returned with the drink, he had become so distracted by what was going on around him he didn't see her coming toward the table.

"Sarah, is this really a whorehouse?" he asked naively and in a voice that was louder than it should have been.

"Keep your voice down, Virdie." She put the drink in front of him and sat down at the table.

"Yes, some men come here for sex, but a lot of them just come to have a drink, listen to music, and relax."

"Why are you here, Sarah?" He grabbed her arm.

She paused and thought about her response. "I've made some really bad mistakes, Virdie. I thought I could work here for a few months, make some fast money, and then move east to the city. But it's not working out that way."

"You shouldn't be here in your condition," he said.

"Maybe not, but I don't have a lot of options to choose from right now." The conversation was making her uncomfortable and fidgety. She twisted her hair nervously around the finger of one hand

and swept the other back and forth across the table in a motion that made it look like she was cleaning it.

"You could come live with me and Mama." He leaned in toward her with urgency. "I could use the help with keeping an eye on her. I'm out working in the fields or the barn most of the day, and she's by herself. She does okay, but I worry about her being alone so much. Her mind is slipping. She'll be eighty-five this spring, you know. Mama always loved you, Sarah. Having a baby in the house would probably do you and her a lot of good."

If Virdie's offer had come a year earlier, Sarah would probably have laughed in his face. Back then, she was excited, full of hope, and bursting at the seams to see what her life could be. The very idea of living in a town where the most exciting entertainment was Saturday night bingo at the fire hall had absolutely no appeal. But a lot had changed in a year. She was tired and feeling like she had lived a dozen lifetimes. A home that was good for the baby, where the two of them would be safe and close to family, now offered some appeal.

"Thanks, Virdie. I'll think about it. I do need somewhere to go once the baby comes."

"You can leave this place right now, Sarah. Come home with me! Let's go!" He grabbed her forearm.

"No, I need to work as long as I can to save money. Right now, I'm waitressing and living in Warren with two of the girls that work here. It's not like being home with Uncle Brady, but it's okay."

"I told Uncle Brady I would come check on you. How in the world am I going to tell him you're pregnant?" Virdie's voice grew loud again. Sarah put her finger to her lips again to hush him.

"I miss Uncle Brady so much. Is he okay? I hope he can be part of this baby's life." She felt herself getting emotional.

"He's fine, but he's worried sick about you. That's why you need to come home with me. You need your family right now." He pulled on her arm again, forceful and insistent.

"Let me think about it, Virdie. But you're right. I do need my family."

Virdie sat and had his drink while Sarah went back and forth between him and the other customers. Iris came down around

9:00 p.m. looking to see what men were there and if any might be interested in coming upstairs. The black dress she wore clung close and tight to her chocolate body like a second skin. Its deep-plunging neckline went well beyond the bottom of her cleavage to reveal the top of her toned stomach. She made her way around the room, laughing and flirting with a few of the men, but none seemed particularly interested; they just wanted to drink. When she got to Virdie, Sarah was in the back, getting something from the storage room.

"Hey, mister, you looking for some company?" She came up from behind him and ran her hand seductively across his shoulders. Virdie was nervous and uneasy. He had never been touched by a colored woman before, let alone have one come on to him. There were only a few Negroes in Ravenna, and he didn't know any of them.

"No, ma'am," he responded, unsure of what to say or what she was asking.

"I can show you a real good time if you wanna come upstairs wit' me," she whispered in his ear. "You got money?"

His dumbfounded expression and the red flush that came over his face spoke of how uncomfortable he was. Before he could answer, Sarah came from the back and saw them. She knew immediately what Iris was doing. It was the typical sporty flirtation that Wallace had taught all of them. "Make 'em want it," he had said.

"Move away, Iris. That's my cousin."

"Your cousin?" Iris drew back and looked at him curiously. "He just looked like another white boy out for a good time to me."

"Well, he's not. He's just here to see me," Sarah responded sharply as she sat down in the chair next to Virdie.

"Whatever," Iris said, irritated. She rolled her eyes the usual way and moved slowly toward the front desk for some conversation with Miss Betty, who, at the time, was focused on her daily newspaper.

"I can't believe you know a woman like that," Virdie said, watching Iris walk away.

"What do you mean a woman like that?" Sarah was immediately upset by his comment. "Is it because she's a colored woman or because she's a prostitute?"

She may not have liked Iris, but she didn't consider herself any better than her, not because she was colored and certainly not because she was a working girl. But she knew Virdie's side of the family were closed-minded racists. She could remember overhearing arguments her mama and his mama had about "the coloreds."

"Lucy, why you let those people in your house is beyond me," she overheard her Aunt Rae say on more than one occasion.

"Come on, Sarah, you know what I mean. Bad enough you're doing god knows what in this place. But with a woman like that…" Virdie stopped himself, realizing he was saying too much.

"A woman like what, Virdie?" She stood to her feet. "I'm a woman like that."

She tightened her face at him. It was clear she was angry.

"Maybe it's time for you to leave."

"Come on, Sarah, I didn't mean nothing by it." Virdie grabbed at her, trying to coax her to sit back down.

"Go home, Virdie," she said sternly. "Thanks for the offer of a place to live. I'll think about it and let you know."

Virdie's behavior was a reminder of the backward attitudes she would have to put up with from him and his mother if she moved to Ravenna. The thought of it made her feel sick to her stomach.

"We're family, Sarah. You need us right now," Virdie pleaded, realizing their conversation had taken a wrong turn.

Sarah grabbed him under the arm and tugged to make him stand to his feet. She walked with him over to the front door, took his hat and coat from the rack, and handed it to him. Her expression was blank when she opened the door and looked at him.

"Please tell Uncle Brady I love him and that I'm okay."

Virdie shook his head disbelievingly while pulling the collar of his coat up around his neck. He headed out into the cold night.

Chapter 22

April 1948

"Push, girl, push!" Miss Betty shouted over Sarah's shoulder as she sat on one side of the bed with both feet planted on the floor for support. The stout woman had assumed a twisted pretzel position, which allowed her to get up close and snug against Sarah's back. Her flabby biceps came up under both of Sarah's armpits and provided a stable brace for her to bear down as the contractions came closer and closer together.

At the other end of the bed was Doc Southall. The wrinkles on his brow were serious. He peered down and over his glasses at what was coming. The sleeves of his crisp shirt were rolled up to the elbow, and he was intent as he inspected the area between her open legs.

"Looks like the top of the head. It won't be long now, Sarah. Breathe in and out slow and steady." He inhaled deep and exhaled fully when demonstrating how she should do it.

⧫

Saturday morning started routinely with breakfast in the kitchen. It was the first time in a long time everybody was present and accounted for at the long table. Bobby started tapping on everyone's door around nine thirty, spreading the word.

"Mama's making her apple pancakes. If you want some, she say you need to hurry on down."

Betty's apple cinnamon pancakes were among her specialties and a huge hit whenever she made them. To top it off, she doused them with warm maple syrup that she also drizzled on the scrambled eggs and sausage she served alongside.

"Miss Betty, you put your foot in these pancakes." Wallace stuffed another forkful into his mouth. He let out a satisfied moan without looking up from his plate. Everyone was enjoying their food with their eyes focused on their plates. Unlike the others, Sarah was struggling to eat the huge helping Miss Betty put on her plate. After the early weeks of terrible morning sickness, she had regained her strength and felt great most of the time. But contrary to most pregnant women, she didn't have much of an appetite. The thought of food or at times, the smell of it, made her nauseous, so she tried to avoid it. Fortunately, Miss Betty kept a watchful eye on her and constantly coaxed her into eating something.

"Little girl, you feeding two mouths now, so you need to eat up." But after only a few bites, Sarah usually found herself feeling stuffed and bloated.

Wallace finished first, then pushed his plate away, and lit a cigarette. He took a deep drag and let go a plume of smoke.

"Everybody, listen up. Looks like we got us a busy night ahead. Ben got word this morning from his brother at the hotel that there's a big group in town for a meeting. Lots of folks asking around about where to go for a good time. Sounds like a bunch of white folks with money to spend. Girls, you need to eat up 'cause this could be a long night."

"Sounds good to me, WB," said Iris, smiling and looking at Shirley. "It's 'bout time this dry spell ended. I need to make some money."

It had been the kind of winter that seemed to go on forever. It was so cold that on some weekends the girls were lucky if they each got one customer. People had chosen to stay inside and close to a warm fire. Another heavy snow in early March had crippled everything, and the dirty remnants of it were still on the ground even though it was April. However, signs of spring were starting to appear. That morning was particularly warm and fresh. Miss Betty had the window open over the sink, and it was letting in a crisp breeze. The yellow muslin curtains flapped while the sound of birds singing in the yard filled the kitchen.

"I'm ready too," said Shirley. "Me and Mama been late with the rent three months in a row, and the landlord said one more time and he's putting us out."

"Now that's what I like to hear," said Wallace. "What about you two?" he said, looking at Loretta and Barbara. "You ready for a busy night?"

"As long as they come with cash, I'm ready." Barbara sounded strictly business, though less excited than Iris and Shirley.

"I'm ready too, WB." Loretta's tone was similar to her sister's.

"Sam and Sarah, make sure you are good and stocked at the bar. Sam, bring those two cases of bourbon in the storage room out from the back 'cause I think we're gonna need them."

They both nodded over their plates, acknowledging his instructions. She and Sam were a solid team. The parlor, music, and the customers downstairs were their domain, along with Ben and Harry, who provided backup and security. Sarah continued to waitress even though she was now well into her eighth month. Wallace had a new uniform specially made for her that was slightly longer but still showed off her lean legs. The black polyester fabric was stylish but draped fully over her body in contrast to her earlier uniform that was much shorter and tight. She had gained very little weight, and when she put her makeup on the way Loretta taught her, she was still as gorgeous as ever. Looking at her, it was difficult to tell if she was pregnant or not. When Wallace saw her in the new uniform for the first time, he said, "Man, you still look good. You sure you're pregnant?" Sarah smiled that he was pleased but sad to think he could make such a joke.

"People will always disappoint you," Reverend Wright had told her once during one of their meetings. He was right, and Wallace was a real-life example.

The relationship they once had was nonexistent. It was painful, but she had finally accepted that the distance between them was a permanent condition. He was the boss, and she was nothing more than one of the girls that worked at the house. Though it was never mentioned again by him or anyone else, she knew the child growing inside her was his, whether he chose to believe it or not.

After breakfast, Sarah walked down to the church. Since that first Saturday months ago, she had gone back to the church several times, hoping to see Reverend Wright. Sometimes he would be there and sometimes he wasn't. He explained that on some Saturdays, he visited with the sick and shut-ins in the congregation. On those Saturdays when he wasn't there, it was just her, the quiet, and the huge cross of Jesus—and He was always there when she sat on the front pew and talked to Him.

When she entered the sanctuary that morning, it was thick with the smell of hymnals, the air of scripture, and the reverent quiet she had come to expect. There was something distinct about the quiet. It generated a stillness on the inside of her she couldn't explain. All the noisy, self-defeating chatter in her head, which constantly condemned, suddenly stopped and kept silent. Her weighty burdens felt lighter, if only for a short time.

In her normal seat on the first pew, right in front of the pulpit, she sat for a long time—her eyes closed, soaking in the stillness and listening. The past eleven months ran over her like a rushing river. It felt more like ten years had passed instead of less than one. She would never have imagined eighteen could feel so old. So many regrets...

I wish I could go back and start over. I should have stayed at the pharmacy, taken odd jobs, and saved every penny. It would have taken longer, but eventually, I would have had enough money and been on my way east and out of this place! Dr. Southall was right. I shouldn't have been in such a hurry. I wish Rita and I had never found 520 that night. I really wish I never met Wallace. I was so stupid! She wiped away tears with the back of her hand.

I could still be living in my room at home with Uncle Brady.

She imagined Brady's face. *And he wouldn't hate me like he does now! I miss him so much.*

She couldn't be sure if or when she would ever be ready to face him again. She cried, praying aloud, "God, please help me make everything right again."

After a few counseling sessions with the reverend, she had decided to go stay with Virdie and his mother once the baby came. It wasn't what she wanted, but it was the only thing that made sense.

In a couple of months, when the baby is old enough, we're leaving for the city, she told herself.

It shouldn't be that hard to get a job as a live-in babysitter for a rich New York family. I can watch their children while taking care of my own.

Finally, she thought she had a plan.

When she was leaving the church around one thirty, a queer twinge ran through her belly. She put her hand on her rounded stomach and rubbed it in a circular motion. It left her a little breathless, so she held onto the railing of the steps until it passed. The baby always moved around a lot, but this seemed different.

I wonder what that was. The last time Dr. Southall examined her, he said she still had a couple more weeks.

Getting back to the house, she came in through the kitchen door, hoping to avoid seeing anyone. The smell of bacon was still lingering, but everything was cleaned and put away, and no one was there. She hurried up the backstairs and went straight to her room, exhausted. She took the grape-colored throw off the back of the chair, lay on the bed, and pulled it up to her neck. A deep sleep quickly consumed her and lasted for hours.

A little before six, she awoke to the same twinge as earlier.

It's probably nothing.

"Please, baby, it's going to be a busy night, and Mama has to work." She talked to her stomach while caressing it.

"Lord, please don't let this baby come tonight," she asked earnestly and desperate.

The pain stopped, and by 6:30, she had convinced herself it was probably just gas resulting from the big breakfast that morning. She dressed in her uniform, combed through her hair, put on her makeup, and was ready to go downstairs by seven.

"How you doing, Miss Sarah?" Sam called out when she hit the bottom step. Even though the two were now like big brother and little sis, he still put miss in front of her name.

179

"I guess I'm okay, Sam," she said, walking toward him. He was using a towel to wipe spotless the glasses that had been washed and set out to dry the night before.

"My stomach has been queasy since breakfast. I think it might be gas or something."

"It's probably all that syrup. You know how heavy-handed Miss Betty is."

He was right. Betty used a ton of syrup on her pancakes.

"Maybe so. All I know is this is not the night for me to be sick." She picked up a towel and began helping him. "I hope working will keep me busy so I won't think about it."

"Okay, but you let me know if you start to feel worse. We got a busy night, but that baby you carrying comes first."

Ben and Harry came from the back, each carrying a cardboard box up on their shoulders. The giant duo was dressed for work in their black suits.

"Where do you want these, Sam?" asked Harry.

"Just put 'em back here on the floor," he said, pointing to a corner behind the bar.

Wallace came out from the back but stopped in the doorway of the hall. He assumed a wide manly stance and put both hands on his hips. He stood and surveyed the downstairs, looking around to see if everything was ready. He was always a snazzy dresser, but in anticipation of a big night, he was particularly sharp. The striking gray suit he wore was made of a material that had a sheen. It looked custom-made to fit his frame. The pinky rings and gold watch he usually wore when he dressed his best added sparkle to his handsome appearance.

"Everything ready to go, Sam?"

"Yeah, boss. We ready."

Sarah was finishing up wiping the glasses while he moved onto unpacking the boxes Ben and Harry delivered.

"Boys, you need to head out front and start keeping an eye on things out there."

"Okay, boss," Ben responded for both of them, and they left out the front door.

"How you doing tonight, Sarah?" Wallace said when he noticed her.

"I'm fine, WB. Don't worry about me."

She was not in the mood for his arrogance, nor did she have the energy to try to engage him. Besides, she had no intention of letting him know what was really going on with her. It was clear his complete focus was on the money he planned to make that night. Anybody or anything that interfered with that would be an unwelcome distraction. He expected everybody to do their part, so she needed to do hers.

"Okay, good!"

She could see he was glad he could count on her.

Miss Betty was busy at the desk going about her routine while Bobby put away folded sheets and towels in the cabinet behind it.

"Everything ready with you, Miss Betty?" Wallace called out to her from across the foyer.

"As ready as we gon' git, Wallace," she said gruffly. "Girls say they ready upstairs too." She pointed up toward the second floor, and Loretta, Barbara, Iris, and Shirley were all lined up across the banister, looking down at them. One just as beautiful as the next with their makeup perfect and all wearing their short pink robes. They were stunning.

"We ready, WB!" Iris shouted loudly, like she was their spokesperson.

"Okay then. Let's make this money!"

By 8:00 p.m., there were already about twenty-five people downstairs. Most of them middle-aged white men in dull dingy-colored suits and crew haircuts. They were different from the usual Saturday night crowd. The intonation in their voices suggested they might have been from somewhere down South—maybe Georgia or the Carolinas. They all appeared to know each other, and the more they drank, the louder they became. Sam put Benny Goodman and a few more he thought they would like on the record player, and the room became charged. He and Sarah were having one of their busiest nights ever.

Shortly after things began to pick up, Sarah got another twang in her stomach, which was followed shortly after by yet another. The second one was more prolonged and a lot more painful. Luckily, it happened while she was standing at the bar, waiting for Sam to fill her tray with orders. She was able to grab on and lean against it without anyone noticing, until the pain passed.

Oh my goodness, Lord, please don't let this baby come tonight was all she could think as she tried to stabilize herself and catch her breath. After Sam finished putting all the drinks on the tray, she lifted it and turned to leave, but both she and the tray were shaky. Miraculously, she managed to get the round of drinks to their rightful owners.

At 9:30, the house was packed. More Negroes were in the crowd than earlier, and a few jazzy-dressed women had joined too. Men of both colors, sizes, and ages were going up and coming down the red stairs in succession. Miss Betty was keeping busy at the desk, and Bobby ran sheets and towels as fast as he could. Everyone was earning their pay. Wallace was here, there, and everywhere throughout the house, making sure the customers were having a good time and were spending their money. He ran into Sarah in the crowd with her tray.

"Everything all right, Sarah?" he asked, passing her on his way somewhere else.

"I'm fine" was all she said and kept moving.

Just minutes before, she had rushed back to the storage room when she felt another wave coming. While in there, she crouched, bent over against the wall, and held her stomach until it was over. After that one, Sarah realized it was more than just gas and began wondering what she should do. At first, she tried to keep serving the customers, but she could feel herself getting weaker and weaker. She decided to tell Sam and struggled to make it through the standing-room-only crowd and back over to the bar. Just as she reached it, the music ended, and a male voice yelled, "Get off me, nigger!" A hush-like gasp ran through the crowd. A dingy suit had stumbled drunk into a colored man.

"Who you callin' nigger, you white cracker!" the man in a red zoot suit said, angry.

"You and your hillbilly friends ain't got no business here anyway. This here is a colored man's whorehouse."

The white one swung at the colored one, and a skirmish began. Ben and Harry immediately moved in to break it up, but chaos broke loose, and a civil war ensued between the dull suits and everyone else. Tables turned over, glasses fell broken to the floor, a chair was split into pieces. Fists, spit, and blood flew everywhere. Wallace and Sam joined Ben and Harry and tried to break up the crowd with little success. There were too many angry people full of alcohol for the four of them to handle.

Finally, a woman screamed at the top of her lungs and yelled, "He's got a knife!"

It got everyone's attention, and the fighting abruptly stopped.

Lying on his back in the middle of the parlor floor was the dingy-suited man who started the fight. Blood was quickly drenching the front of his white shirt and running onto the floor. It was hard at first to tell who had done it because the man he got into the fight with looked as bewildered and confused as everyone else.

"It was him!" one of the suits said, pointing to another colored man in the crowd who was holding a bloody blade. When they identified him, he stood frozen, looking guilty and scared. He dropped the knife, quickly turned, pushed his way through the crowd, and ran out the front door.

When he was out of sight, one of the drab suits yelled, "Let's get him!" And most of the whites rushed out into the night after him. The others that remained sensed it was time to go and promptly left. The only ones that stayed were the man who lay dying or dead and two of his dreary-suited companions who were trying to attend to him.

During the confusion, Sarah crouched down behind the bar to stay out of the way. Three more of what she now realized were contractions had come over the twenty minutes or so she was hiding. The last one was so intense she lay helpless and whimpering in a fetal position on the highly trafficked floor.

"Miss Sarah, you all right!" Sam looked worried when he discovered her that way.

"Sam, the baby is coming!" She stayed tucked in a ball and held her hand out toward him for him to take it. He kneeled beside her to see what he could do.

"I'm scared, Sam."

Just then, she felt a trickle and knew it was her water breaking.

"Don't you worry 'bout nothing. I got you covered." Sam grabbed her up from the floor. She wasn't heavy, but his bad leg made it hard for him to keep steady while holding her.

"I need some help over here." He called over to where Wallace, Ben, and Harry were still standing around, looking at the man lying on the floor, trying to figure out what needed to happen next. Wallace looked up to see Sam carrying Sarah in his arms and struggling not to drop her.

"What the hell!" He was shocked at what he saw and rushed over to help him.

"She's having the baby, boss."

"Are you kidding me!" he said angrily, looking at Sarah writhing in pain. "What else can go wrong tonight!" He put both his open palms to the sides of his head and shook it.

"Miss Betty, we need your help over here," Wallace called out and took Sarah from Sam's arms as Miss Betty rushed over to see what was the matter.

"Lawd, this child ain't having that baby now, is she?"

"I'll take her up to her room, but I need you to stay with her," he told her. "Too much going on down here."

"All right, all right!" she mumbled as she followed him.

From the top of the stairs, Betty shouted, "Sam, dial up Doc Southall and tell him we need him over here as quick as he can. We got plenty business for him tonight."

Chapter 23

"Doc, you performed another miracle. Looks like that guy is gonna make it," Wallace was excited when he talked to Doc through the crack he was holding in the door to Sarah's room, barely looking inside.

The last thing he wanted was for the news to get out that a customer had been murdered at *520*. It would be bad for business, and the police would be swarming all over the place, asking questions.

❧

Doc Southall had arrived at 11:45 p.m. and immediately went to work on the man bleeding on the parlor floor. He pulled a bottle of disinfectant from his bag, gave him some sort of shot, and then tightly wrapped the deep wound in his stomach with gauze.

"He needs blood," said Doc after he had done all he could do.

Ben and Harry, along with his two companions, carefully put him on the back seat of Wallace's Buick. To minimize a scandal, they agreed it would be better if Harry drove them to Youngstown Hospital since he, as well as his buddies, were white.

"You should take them. Less likely the hospital will call the cops if they don't see a Negro," Ben said while helping load the man with his exposed gauze-wrapped white belly into the back of the car.

"No problem. I understand. Tell the boss it's taken care of," said Harry.

When Harry got back to the house later, he gave Wallace the good news. "That guy's buddies were not interested in getting the police involved either," he joked to Wallace.

"They didn't want to risk having to explain to them or their wives back home what they were doing here in the first place."

∼∽

"Glad it all worked out, nephew," Doc responded through the door. "I've got my hands busy with this one right now."

Sarah screamed with agony as another contraction ripped through her body.

"Is she gonna be all right?" said Wallace, leaning in close to the door. The emotion in his voice was faint but detectable.

"She'll be fine, son. It's just Mother Nature at work. Won't be long now."

"Ughhhhhhhh!" Sarah wailed.

"Let me know when it's done, Miss Betty."

"I sho' will, Wallace. Now go tend to the rest of the house."

He closed the door and went back downstairs.

The other girls all heard Sarah screaming and had gathered out in the hallway, standing around waiting, dressed in their shiny pink. Customer traffic up to the second level came to a halt when Betty left the desk to come upstairs.

"This is just like Anna all over again!" Shirley remembered that night four years ago. "Sarah's sounds just like Anna," she said.

She looked at Iris, and both their faces grimaced with pain every time Sarah's screams rang out down the hallway.

"It figures, white girl would have that baby at the worst possible time," said Iris.

"Shut up, Iris!" Barbara yelled. "She couldn't control when the baby came."

Sarah let go of another gut-wrenching scream. It rang top to bottom and around the big house and was accompanied by Miss Betty yelling, "Push, girl, push!"

Iris didn't like the way Barbara came back at her. "That white broad has been nothing but a pain in my butt since she got here," she said loudly.

"I knew she was going to be trouble the first time I put eyes on her."

"You're just mad because WB likes her," Loretta said, pointing at Iris and smiling. "Colored men can say what they want, but they like white skin touching theirs."

Iris got really mad at Loretta and rushed toward her, ready to fight.

"Take it easy, Iris," Shirley said, holding her back. "These two heifers are just tryin' us."

At that moment, they heard a clapping noise that sounded like the baby's backside being slapped. It was followed shortly after by the dissatisfied wailing of a newborn. Wallace heard the crying from below and ran up the stairs two at a time and burst into the room.

"Lawd, look at this here!" Miss Betty was grinning ear to ear, watching Doc holding the crying infant.

Betty didn't even sound like herself. The sight of the beautiful baby girl with a full head of reddish-brown hair had immediately softened her. Doc took the baby over to the bureau where he used instruments from his bag to weigh and measure her and then wrapped her in a clean white linen cotton. Wallace came and moved in close so he could get a good look. He put his hand on Doc's shoulder and looked over and smiled at the tiny little person he was handling.

Sarah was exhausted and out of it. She was so drained after the final push that she didn't really get a chance to see her new daughter. While Doc worked on the baby, Miss Betty helped get Sarah cleaned up. She could be skillful in such situations and masterfully changed the sheets on the bed with Sarah still in it. After the cleanup and a few minutes to regain her strength, Sarah was sitting upright in the bed.

"Doc, can I see my baby?" She extended both arms in his direction. He brought the neatly tucked bundle over and put the baby in her arms. Sarah planted a delicate kiss on the child's forehead and took extra time to breathe in the smell of her hair and her innocence.

Wallace pulled up a chair next to the side of the bed, and for a moment, he and Sarah looked at each other and smiled, both gazing at the sweetness of the little girl quietly sleeping. Miss Betty and Doc sensed their need for privacy. So they gathered everything up and left the room.

"I'm going to name her Patty Jean," Sarah told him when they had gone.

"That's nice. I think it fits her." Wallace's strong demeanor seemed to temporarily evaporate as he lightly stroked the soft skin of the baby's tiny hand.

For a few minutes, it was as if they were a family.

"If this is my baby, Sarah, she ain't growing up in this place," he told her. "You not ready to take care of a child." His tone began to change. "I don't know why you ever thought you were. It didn't have to be like this. I could have handled it."

"Handle what, WB? This is our baby!" Frustrated, she paused and secured the white cloth around the baby. "Don't worry, I don't need anything from you. The baby and me, we will be fine on our own."

"I'm not having her wandering around with no place to call home. She needs to be somewhere she can be taken care of, like a child of mine is supposed to be." Wallace looked at the baby and touched her cheek.

As arrogant as he sounded, she was glad to hear he was finally accepting the fact that she was his daughter until, of course, he said what was really on his mind...

"You can go on with your life, Sarah. Go live that New York dream you told me about."

"What are you saying, WB?"

"I'll take her. It'll be like this never happened." He stood up and gently tugged the baby from Sarah's arms.

"Wait! What are you doing?" She reached, grabbing for the child but careful and afraid of hurting her. Quick and without apology, Wallace headed toward the door with the bundle in his arms.

"No!" she screamed. "Please don't take her! WB, I'm begging you, please! She's my baby! She needs me!"

"You gotta trust me, Sarah," he said, looking at her. "It's better for her this way. She doesn't belong here."

"Where are you taking her?" Sarah pulled back the covers and put her feet on the floor to stand up.

"Somewhere she can have a good life with people who can take care of her. Don't worry. Just forget about it."

"No! Please!" she cried. She stood shakily, lurching to try to stop him. But he left quickly with the baby and closed the door.

Chapter 24

On Sunday, the house was quiet, but all the trauma from the night before remained. Everyone had heard Sarah's screaming when Wallace took the baby and knew that she was now holed up in her room, alone and devastated. In the early afternoon, Loretta and Barb stopped by to see how she was and to see if she felt well enough to head back to Warren with them. Sarah was deep under the covers when they came in.

"You okay, Sarah?" Loretta asked tenderly as she tapped lightly on the door while opening it and walking in. It was early afternoon, but the closed curtains were letting in very little light. The room was shadowy and dark and had a faint yet detectable clinical aroma that signaled something out of the ordinary had happened there. Sarah sat up gradually as she was sore.

Loretta and Barb took turns hugging the girl they had come to accept as a little sister. Barb took the pillows and one by one fluffed and put them behind Sarah's back so she could comfortably sit up and talk to them.

"I'm okay," she said, her voice low and raspy from not having spoken a word since last night. Barb and Loretta sat on opposite sides at the foot of the bed.

"We came to look in on you and see if you feel up to going home with us today?" said Barb; she rubbed at Sarah's leg beneath the lavender cover. There was a long pause while they waited for her to say something.

"I don't think I can leave here yet." Her voice was soft and cracking.

"This is where I held her and kissed her and smelled her hair. And now she's gone." Her voice was low, and every word drenched in sadness.

Sarah looked at the two of them and then off into space, like she was seeing everything happen all over again. Her eyes glistened and then overflowed. Barb and Loretta moved close around and hugged and held her and let her cry for as long as she needed.

"We understand, Sarah. If you decide tomorrow or the next day you want to come home, just dial me up, and I'll come get you, okay?" Loretta stroked the back of Sarah's hand.

"Thank you, Loretta. I'll let you know." She wiped at her eyes and nose with her fists.

"We're here for you, Sarah. You don't have to go through this by yourself," said Barb.

After they left, Sarah slouched back down in the bed and pulled the covers up over her head. A short time later, Sam was tapping at the door.

"Miss Sarah, you all right in there?" he asked, concerned.

"I'm okay, Sam. I just need to sleep and be myself." From under the covers, her voice was muffled and soft.

She didn't like turning Sam away, but truth was, she didn't feel up to conversation.

"All right then," he said. "Ughh, I'm gettin' ready to go on home, but I wanted to make sure you were all right before I left."

Sam leaned his head against the door, waiting for her to answer.

"I'm okay. Thank you for checking on me." Her voice was sweet. "I'll see you next week, okay, Sam?"

Her words were drained of energy, but there was also a faint flitter of uncertainty when she spoke about next week. If today was like any other Sunday morning and the weekend was ending, like always, then of course she would see him next week. But this Sunday wasn't like all the other Sunday mornings. Everything was different now, and she wasn't sure where she was going to be tomorrow, let alone next week.

"Okay then, well, take care of yourself now, ya hear?" He paused, listening at the door to see if he could hear anything.

"Love you, Miss Sarah," he said quietly against the wood. "Love you too, Sam. Thank you."

∂∽∂

For four days, Sarah stayed up in her room. Miss Betty checked on her at least twice a day and brought food up, but she barely touched it. When Wednesday came, she was still in bed, and Betty's patience had run out.

"It's time for you to get up, little girl," she said as she burst into the room around ten that morning. She carried folded white sheets and had a towel and washcloth over her arm. The curtains had been drawn since Saturday night when the baby came, so Miss Betty headed straight for the window and gathered up one in either hand and snatched them open wide to let in a sunny spring morning. Sarah stirred and began to sit up in the bed, startled by all the commotion she was making. Squinting her eyes, she tried to adjust to the light. She pulled her blond hair, getting it out of her face.

"I know you hurtin' and everything. But life got to go on."

Miss Betty pulled at Sarah's arm to coax her to get up and then put her arm around her waist to help move her from the bed to the corner chair in order to change the linens. She was still wearing the white flannel nightgown she had on when she held her perfect baby girl for the first time.

"If I let everythin' that tried to knock me down to my knees in life keep me there, I woulda been dead and gone a long time ago." She pulled off the cases from the two pillows and powerfully ripped the sheets from the bed down to the mattress. Sarah sat quiet and fragile, listening intently to the woman she always thought hated her.

"You young, you still got your whole life ahead. You can't let this keep you knocked down. You strong. I seen it." She tucked and folded the bottom sheet into the corners of the bed with the expertise of a nurse. "You came in here green and was one of these girls faster than anybody I ever seen."

It was a backhanded compliment, but Sarah remembered how determined she had been to do a good job. How she had been so willing to do whatever it took to make the money. It wasn't the kind of example of being strong she could be proud of, but she was beginning to see Miss Betty's point.

"You just need to get up and pull yourself together." She finished making the bed and went over to the chair where Sarah was sitting. Miss Betty bent over at the waist, took hold of both arms of the chair, and put her face so close to Sarah's that she could smell her breath.

"You hearing me?" she spoke forcefully and sharp, and Sarah was shaken by it.

"Yes, ma'am, I-I-I hear," she stuttered.

Just as Miss Betty was finishing up and getting ready to leave, Sarah was hesitant but mustered the courage to ask, "Miss Betty, do you know where Wallace took my baby?" she asked desperately.

Miss Betty's face went blank, like the question had taken her by surprise. She fumbled around and moved slowly when gathering up the dirty linens in her arms. There was an awkward silence.

"You don't have to worry none 'bout that baby," she finally said in her Southern way. "There's more to Wallace than you can see wit' the eye. His mama and Doc Southall, they brother and sister. My guess is she wit' them."

Sarah was shocked yet relieved to think that might be where he had taken her.

"Them folks got money, so she gon' be all right."

The conversation with Miss Betty encouraged Sarah and helped her begin to shake off the dazed stupor she was in. Gradually, she realized she couldn't provide little Patty with the kind of life Wallace's family could. She had to figure out her own life first; she didn't even have a permanent place to call home. To bring a child, so dependent on her, into that kind of lack didn't seem fair.

Wallace has his faults, but he won't let anything happen to our daughter. Her mind began to settle at the thought.

She washed up, put on a clean gown, and returned to the chair in the corner. There she cuddled up with her grape blanket and sat all day, peering out the window at the world. She was mindful and silent. Her mama, Brady, Rita, Sister Anne, and Reverend Wright all, one by one, eventually made their way out of the fog and into the foreground of her mind. She wondered what each would say if they could see her now. She sat, eyes closed, laboring over the mess she had made. After a long while, she began to pray aloud and from the heart.

"God, I've made so many mistakes. I'm sorry I messed up. But I know in my heart, You still love me. I prayed, and You convinced me to keep Patty Jean. I didn't think I would ever be able to do it by myself, but You kept me strong. God, after all that, I can't believe I have to lose her!" She wiped at her face with the sleeve of her gown. "I want to do what's right for her. Please watch over my sweet little girl."

Her heart surged, remembering the baby's face and the overwhelming love she felt during the few minutes she got to hold her.

When Thursday morning came, she was feeling stronger. There was still no sign of Wallace. He had been unaccounted for since Saturday night. Once or twice she could have sworn she heard his voice downstairs, but he never came up to check in on her. Tomorrow was Friday, and another busy *520* weekend would be gearing up, so she decided it was time to go.

Sarah packed her things and dressed in a modest beige skirt and navy sweater and all the while worried about what she should do or where she should go. Continuing to stay at *520* after everything that happened made no sense. A return to the sporting life was completely out of the question, and she couldn't imagine herself as a waitress for the rest of her life. It had been nearly a year since that night, last spring, when she and Rita took the bus to Youngstown on a journey of discovery and wound up at *520*. Sarah got mad and began throwing her clothes into her suitcase, thinking how naive she had been.

"How could I be so stupid!"

In a year's time, she had changed more than some people do their whole life. She had become a different person and was desperate to make amends for all her bad choices. She closed the suitcase and sat down on the bed to consider her options.

Moving in with Eugene and her aunt Rae wouldn't work either. She was willing to make the sacrifice for the baby, but without her, she would never be able to live under the same roof with them and their backward, bigoted ways.

Then she remembered the several hundred dollars she had in the coffee can under her bed at Loretta and Barb's house. Standing to her feet, she looked at herself in the mirror on the dresser.

Maybe now's my chance to get out of here! I can try to forget any of this ever happened.

She was scared but anxious to think she might still have a chance to find the life she hoped was out there waiting.

It's now or never! I know I have at least enough saved to buy a ticket to Grand Central and still have a little money left until I can find a job. She filled with hope even though she had no idea where she would go or where she would stay once she got there.

The tears came again when she thought about how different everything turned out from the way it was supposed to be. She should have been leaving the house with her new baby in tow—and not alone.

When she was ready to go, Sarah listened at the door for the house to be quiet. About one o'clock, she tiptoed down the steps, suitcase in hand, and went out the front door and out into a warm sunny afternoon. She hurried out the gate and onto the street, hoping not to be seen by anyone. Her new plan was to catch the bus back to Warren and Loretta and Barb's house. She would gather up a few things, get the money from under the bed, and be on her way the next day. She considered calling Loretta to come get her like she offered, but it had been four days, and it just seemed too much to ask. Tomorrow she would catch the noon bus to Pittsburgh. From there, she would get on the Greyhound, and by Saturday evening, she would be among the tall buildings in Manhattan and far away from all that haunted her. She was terrified, but it was the only plan she could come up with that made any sense.

The mile walk back to the bus stop where she and Rita had gotten off that first night was familiar. The bar on the corner where the two white men had shouted at them was closed, but she remembered how the loud one had yelled and told them they needed to go home.

I wish I had listened.

What she didn't remember along the walk was the pharmacy she now saw across the street. It was small and with a barely notice-able red sign out front that read *Woodrow's Drugs* in white letters. The discovery of it sparked an idea in her head that turned on like a light bulb.

I wonder if that pharmacist knows Doctor Southall? Youngstown isn't that big. Maybe somebody in there knows him.

It was a random idea, but she was wildly curious at the possibility.

There was still twenty-five minutes before the 2:00 bus to Warren came, so she crossed the street and went inside. It was a com-pact store, and only two customers were mulling around through the aisles. Sarah walked straight through the first aisle and along the shelves filled with aspirin and other pills, all the way to the rear drug counter.

"Yes, young lady. How can I help you?" the pale bald pharma-cist in a short white coat asked when he came to the window to see what she needed.

"Ugh, yes, sir, I just got here from Pittsburgh, and my mother told me we have family here. She said it was her second cousin on her father's side." Sarah was being particularly articulate.

"She said I should stop by and say hello to them while I'm in town. Mother said he's a doctor. Southall is the family name. I'm not sure where they live, but I thought maybe since you were a pharma-cist and everything, you might know him?"

"Oh, sure," he said, appearing delighted to hear about the fam-ily connection. "Everybody 'round here knows Doc Southall. You're a cousin, you say?"

"Yes, sir, on my mother's side. You wouldn't happen to know where he lives, would you?"

"Well, I wouldn't normally give out that kind of information, but since you're family, I don't see why not." He reached under the counter and pulled out a leather-bound ledger and started flipping through the pages.

"I know I have Doc's address in here somewhere." He turned page after page as Sarah stood watching him and trying to contain how nervous she was.

"Oh, here it is." He reached for a pen and piece of notepaper and wrote down the address and handed it to her: *1953 Brighton Road.*

"If you head straight down Livingston for about two miles and turn left on Walnut, you'll run right into Brighton Road."

"Thank you so much!" she beamed with gratitude.

"Certainly. I'm always happy to see family staying in touch with each other. It does my heart good. You tell Doc Southall Bill Woodrow sends his regards."

"I will, Mr. Woodrow. Thank you again, sir." Sarah's heart was racing as she hurriedly exited the front door.

Looking at the piece of paper with the address on it created a situation she hadn't counted on. She was supposed to be on her way back to Warren. Yet with little hesitation, she quickly put aside that plan in the hope of seeing Patty Jean and started out on a long walk to find her.

After a half mile, she found herself journeying away from town and toward sleepy rows of houses that felt Middle America and safe. But her suitcase was growing heavy, like a lead weight, and her energy was draining away. It had only been five days since she gave birth, and her body was letting her know it was still sore and tired. Exhaustion slowed her pace to that of a snail's, each step harder than the last. Hopelessness started to set in.

Why am I doing this anyway? I should turn around, head for Warren, and just let this be.

Her mind and body were spent, and she didn't think she was going to be able to make it. About that time, a blue Studebaker drove past and pulled off to the side of the road just ahead of her. A perky young woman, her brunette hair waving in the wind, stuck her head out the driver's side window and looked back at Sarah.

"Miss are you, okay?" she shouted.

She had obviously noticed how labored and slow Sarah was walking and stopped out of concern.

"Yes, ma'am, I'm okay. Just a little tired," Sarah yelled.

"Do you need a lift somewhere? I'm going about two miles up the road. I'd be happy to drop you someplace."

The invitation of a ride was music to Sarah's ears. *Thank you, baby Jesus!*

"Yes, ma'am, if you don't mind. I would love a ride."

"Well come on, hop in."

Sarah got a burst of energy and rushed to get in the car.

"Where you headed?" the lady asked nicely. The back seat of the car was packed with sacks of potatoes, flour, and other supplies, like she had just come from the market.

"Just up to the intersection at Walnut Road," said Sarah.

"No problem. I pass right by there on my way home."

As they rode, the nosy lady pried her with questions about where she was from and where she was going. Sarah, exhausted, was annoyed by all the questioning. She ended up telling her the same story she had given the pharmacist: that she was on her way to see her mother's cousin, Dr. Southall. The woman didn't know him but was familiar with the family name.

"The Southalls own lots of property around Youngstown. My sister rents her place from one of the brothers." The comment added to Sarah's growing awareness of what a well-to-do family the Southalls were. She felt satisfied thinking that Patty Jean would be part of it.

I can't give her that kind of life.

"This is Walnut," the lady said as the car approached the intersection. She brought the car to a stop on the side of the road.

"Thank you so much," Sarah said when getting out of the car.

"Good luck finding your family," said the woman. She steered the car back onto the road and was gone.

Sarah walked across Lexington to take the left on Walnut like Mr. Woodrow told her. She found herself entering a neighborhood that bellowed abundance with its well-kept Victorian homes. Neatly tended flower beds filled by spring tulips and pink azaleas added splashes of color to the professional look of the manicured lawns. They were homes that epitomized success, just like the ones that made the covers of *Better Homes and Gardens* magazine. Her eyes were big as she walked slowly past each one, imagining what it would be like to grow up in a neighborhood with houses like this.

I can't believe people actually live like this right here in Youngstown. She was wide-eyed with amazement.

One house had a massive stone chimney in front with enormous stained glass windows on either side of it. It was stunning. Sarah dropped her mouth as she stopped and gazed. Huge maple trees lined both sides of the street. They were lush and touched in the middle, creating a shady, idyllic scene that beckoned an artist's brush.

At the next cross street, she saw a little sign with Brighton Road on it. She pulled the slip of paper from the pocket of her skirt to confirm the house number again: *1953.*

Already moving slowly from exhaustion, panic also set in when she realized she had no idea what she would do when she got to the house. All that had consumed her was seeing her baby. If Doc opened the door, he would know why she was there, and that could cause a terrible scene. If Wallace's mother came to the door, what would she say?

What would I do? She had no clue.

It was nearing 4:00, but the heavy shade from the trees gave the appearance that it was much later. Approaching number 1953, she got a glimpse of a lamplight, already turned on and shining through a side window. When she was one house away, Sarah turned and looked both ways, up and down the street. Not seeing anyone, quickly but cautiously, she sneaked around the left side of the yard. She took cover with her suitcase in the thickets of the dense ivy that covered the ground and grew up the side of the house. She peered through the window to get a better look.

The inside was spacious and grand with a large foyer and parlor. And in many ways, it was similar in design to *520.* It had the same wide carpeted staircase, but this one was the color hunter green. The light coming through the window was from a lamp on a marble table that was near the stairs. The sitting parlor was classically decorated but looked comfortable with its settee sofa and two high-back chairs.

Unlike *520*, it had the appearance of a home and not a place where men came to satisfy their fantasies.

Sarah stretched her neck to see what she could through the window. Someone apparently played the piano because there was one sitting back in one of the corners. On a far wall, she could see a grouping of family pictures. The distance made it hard to see, but squinting, she made out that a few of them were of Wallace. In one, he looked much younger and was posing on horseback. The photos were a mix of people, young and old, with different complexions—mainly white but brown and ebony too.

After a few minutes, a woman dressed in a lounging gown slowly descended the steps holding a bundle in a pink blanket. The gown was blue like the color of the sky and striking against her porcelain skin. With her graying ginger hair, she looked much like Rita Hayworth. She was beautiful. A softness in her eyes when she looked down and smiled at the covered package in her arms spoke of kindness and grace.

Sarah couldn't see the child's face but recognized the reddish-brown hair sticking out the top of the blanket. She was overcome knowing it was Patty and immediately flashed back to the kiss on the top of the head she gave her the night she was born.

The woman disappeared with the baby to the back of the house. A short time later, she returned with the child in one arm and a small bottle of milk in the other hand. She sat down in a white rocking chair next to the piano. Careful and lovingly, she loosened the blanket around the baby. She squirted a little of the milk from the bottle on the back of her hand and, when satisfied with the temperature, put the bottle to the infant's mouth. As the little girl eagerly sucked, the woman relaxed back into the chair and began to rock. Sarah could hear the faint sound of humming but didn't know the song. Whatever the tune, it was soothing and sweet.

Watching them together, so natural, Sarah's eyes filled and overflowed. As much as she wanted to storm the house and demand to take her child, it was clearer to her than ever that she couldn't afford the life these people would be able to give her. Patty Jean was content, happy, and safe, sucking on a bottle, staring into the eyes of a woman who likely was her grandmother.

Sarah stayed crouched at the window, peeking at them through the ivy. When the bottle was empty, the woman placed it on the edge of the piano and put the blanketed baby over her shoulder and gently patted her back. She hummed the same song and rocked. There was a sweetness in the way she patted and stroked the baby's back. Sarah could see that her daughter was somewhere she was loved. She considered her own life and wondered how different things might be right now if she had been given half the opportunity Patty Jean was surrounded by.

When the baby was burped and had fallen back to sleep, the mature red-haired lady got up and took her back upstairs. When they were out of sight, Sarah slid down the wall of the house, landing on the ground. She stared stunned as if she'd seen a vision.

The best thing for Patty is to leave her here. She deserves this life, and I can't give it to her. Wallace was right. It's not fair to put her through the mess I've made of everything.

An hour passed with her hidden in the thick ivy. She waited to see if there would be any more movement coming from inside the house. When there wasn't and she was satisfied she had seen all there was to see, Sarah wiped her face with the sleeve of her sweater, gathered up her suitcase, and walked befogged back down the shaded street toward Walnut Road. If ever there was a day she would never forget, it would be this one.

It was almost 5:30. The early spring evening was bright and warm, but the heavy shade covering Brighton made it look much later. In her defeated state, she could barely put one foot in front of the other. She was oblivious to her surroundings. Part of her wanted to turn around and go get her daughter, regardless of the consequences. Yet still another part was telling her that walking away was the right thing to do.

Turning onto Walnut Road, she began to emerge from under the cover of the shady maple trees and into the sun. The further she distanced from the house, the more the trance she was drowning in began to lift. She imagined a day in the future when she would see her daughter again. She couldn't be sure when that day would be or if it would ever come. But if it did, she vowed to do everything in her power to make her understand why she left.

Dear Lord, please make her understand that I did it for her, she prayed.

The walk back to Lexington Street, and the stop where she would catch the bus back to Warren seemed like a journey that would never end. No one stopped like before to offer her a ride, which was fine, because she was in no mood to talk to anybody. Luckily, most of the way back was downhill, but still, she was drained and bleary. Her lower back and legs ached, and the suitcase she had been carrying all day was heavier than ever. Luckily, the next bus to Warren was already coming down the street when she got to the stop. She got on behind two older Negro ladies dressed in gray and white maids' uniforms. Both moved slow and seemed tired from the day. They were talking to each other as they boarded the bus, so Sarah couldn't help but overhear their conversation.

"They don't pay me enough to put up with those spoiled rotten children they got. They so disrespectful," the first one said to the other, sounding disgusted.

"Some folks ain't got no business wit' children," said the other woman.

While Sarah waited for them to deposit their coins, she felt pain from the last woman's comment, as though it was meant for her.

Finding an empty seat in the middle of the bus, she sat alone and looked blankly out the window. As the bus pulled away from the curve, she dreamed of coming back someday to find her child after having lived in New York and becoming a famous runway model. Patty Jean would be so proud of her. She would be all grown up by then but still overjoyed to finally see her mama. She was warmed by the thought of a beautiful young girl with brown pigtails running into her arms. How they would hug each other so tight! At least she hoped that's the way it would be.

The day had been long, and she was weary, so she rested her head against the window and, within minutes, was drifting off to sleep. As she did, she remembered everything she had been through and seen that day and, most profoundly, the image of her baby girl content in the arms of a redheaded stranger.

The End

Epilogue

A blistering July sun was beating down on the concrete platform while she sat and waited on a bench for the train to arrive. A few other people were straggled about, doing the same. Some appeared to be, like she was, waiting for someone to arrive while others, with suitcases in hand, obviously were headed to other places and waiting to board. A woman and a young boy, who couldn't have been more than four, sat down next to her on the bench. The little boy was fidgety and impatient.

"Mama, it's hot! Can we go?" He leaped from the bench and pulled at her hand.

"It won't be too long now, Paulie," she told him. "The train will be here with Grandma any minute, and then we can go."

The lady and the little boy were only minor distractions. Her mind was focused on what she would do and say when the trained pulled in, and she saw her face-to-face for the first time.

After about fifteen minutes, waiting in the sweltering sun, the *toot-toot!* of a train whistle could be heard close in the distance. Slowly, a locomotive began pulling into the station. She was excited but, at the same time, terrified to finally see the person she should have known well but knew little about.

When the train stopped and the doors opened, the platform quickly became thick with people getting off while others stood waiting to get on. Hugs and greetings were exchanged as couples were reunited; a family excited to see each other after a long time laughed and smiled together. A young sailor in his navy blues and white cap, holding a bouquet of yellow flowers, grinned wide when he spotted his girl step from the train. When she also saw him, the two of them ran into each other's arms. They kissed and hugged.

Paulie saw his grandmother through the crowd and took off running down the platform excited, yelling, "Grandma! Grandma!"

Gradually, the rush of arriving and departing activity began to diminish, and the platform was nearly empty. She kept looking, searching the faces of every female she saw, but none of them fit the description. She began wondering—maybe they got their signals crossed, and her arrival was actually next Saturday and not this one. But just when it seemed everyone who was going to get off the train had done so, one last female passenger came rushing out and on to the platform. With a suitcase in her left hand, she fumbled with a piece of paper that she held in her right, trying to read what was on it. Though she seemed clumsy, she was a glamorous sight. Lean and beautiful, she wore a well-proportioned purple dress and lavender pillbox hat. The rosy blush on her cheeks and the red of her lips were the perfect touches of makeup on her pale skin. As fetching as she appeared, unless she was on her way to a wedding or some other nice affair, she was overdressed for an average Saturday afternoon in a Midwestern town.

Was that her? Squinting her eyes, she couldn't be certain. She pulled the only photo she had from the side pocket of her skirt and closely compared the photo with the lady standing downwind on the platform. When the last few people had gone and the two of them were the last ones remaining, their eyes naturally met. They looked puzzled at each other, neither of them knowing for sure. Still uncertain but eager to find out, she moved toward her quickly.

Waving her hand, she shouted, "Miss Ruford?"

About the Author

Nobody's Child is the author's debut novel. Karen believes part of her purpose is to encourage, to listen, and offer empathic support to others. *Nobody's Child* is consistent with that mission with the reminder that mistakes and setbacks in life are inevitable, but it's how we grow and learn from those experiences that ultimately determines where our journeys will take us.

While writing has long been her passion, much of Karen's professional career has been spent engaged in strategies aimed to improve America's under-resourced communities and the lives of the people who live there.

She has a graduate degree in English and Creative Writing from Southern New Hampshire University.

A breast-cancer survivor; she lives with her husband, Richard, in Northern Virginia. She is mom to Tenille and Brandi and Gigi to Caiden and Ronen.

CPSIA information can be obtained
at www.ICGtesting.com
Printed in the USA
LVHW030744100921
697444LV00005B/382